THE VILLAGE SCHOOL

ANEZI OKORO

Contents

1

"Present Sir!

"Class up!" the monitor ordered. Everybody sprang smartly to attention.

"Salute!"

The whole class chorused: "Good morning, Sir."

"G' morning," the teacher *drawled*.

"Class sit!" the monitor ordered again. They all sat down amidst the screeching of benches and creaking of desk tops.

The teacher's table had been arranged as neatly as Bassey, the best class monitor in the Central School Amanzu, knew how. The teacher opened the register, which was right in front of him, with his usual *flourish* while *sweeping the rows of each seat with his eyes.*

"Zaccheus Agu."

Present, Sir!'

"Shadrach Banigo!"

"Present, Sir!'

"Bartemius Eke."

"Present, Sir!"

David Eze, David Eze

"Absent, Sir!" someone answered.

"Where is he? I say, where is the fool?"

"Sir, he went with his father to the Uburu salt market to

buy salt."

"Olatunji Johnson."

"Present, Sir!"

"Aaron Kanu."

"Present, *Sir*!"

"Ishmael Kanu... Ishmael Kanu! Aron, where is your brother?"

"Sir, I think he will be coming. After we returned from examining our fish lines this morning, he went to check his rabbit traps. I have given up rabbit trapping myself since I was bitten by a trapped rabbit."

"That's enough... Monitor, put down his name. Three strokes when he arrives. Rabbit traps, my foot!"

"Israel Nwandu."

"Present, Sir!"

"Mark Obike."

"Present, Sir!"

"Ikechukwu Ogbuehi. Ikechukwu Ogbuehi! Where is that unbaptised pagan?"

"Sir, no one knows. I don't think anyone from his village is in school today. Perhaps the bamboo bridge across the Ilo river is broken again," Bassey *volunteered*.

"Abel Okike."

"Present, Sir!"

"Bassey Okike."

"Present, Sir!"

"That's a good boy. Frederick Osisiogu."

"Present, Sir!"

So it went on until Adeyemi Williams had been called. Then, as was the order of things, the turn of the girls came.

"Dorcas Abosi."

"Present, Sir!"

"That's a good girl. Mary Ikedinachi."
Adanma Nweke, Grace Oji, Abigal Onouha. I
am sure you are all present.

"Yes, Sir!" they chorused.

Mr D. S. Okehi was not one to allow
slackness to go unnoticed. His running
commentary during the roll call was not enough.
He proceeded to tell his class (not for the first
time!) about the evils of *sloth* and laziness,
quoting freely from the Bible and from ***John
Ploughman's Talks***. To his credit, however, he
also gave praise where and when it was due. So
after his sermon about absenteeism and
lateness, he turned once more to his monitor
Bassey, who, he claimed, had no absent mark in
his three years in that school. Finally, it was the
turn of his "five 'ever' present girls to be lauded

to the skies. Their faces were hidden behind their exercise books, partly to escape the *scowls* and the unspoken threats from the boys, but largely to hide their embarrassment at the teacher's innocent but *unabashed* excesses.

By this time the classes in *adjacent* rooms were *convulsed* with laughter because Mr D.S. Okhei's voice, whether in *denunciation* or in praise, was very loud indeed; and the classrooms were separated only by low walls, popularly known as dwarf walls.

The roll call over, methodical and *fastidious* Mr Okehi turned to the next stage of his morning routine. He called on Bassey, the class monitor, to collect the homework while he fondly patted the bundle of canes which the class monitor had laid neatly on the right-hand corner of his table. To Mr Okehi, the cane was a very important part of the teaching method. He believed that it was responsible for the girls' punctuality, that it ensured that pupils did their homework and that it helped them to think clearly during lessons. Bassey dutifully collected the open exercise books, one on the top of the other, and laid them on the teacher's table. The homework was Arithmetic, but happily for Abigail and her girlfriends, and also for most of the boys, their teacher had rearranged his time-table so that Arithmetic was the third lesson instead of the first as in most other classes. No one was sure why he did it. Some thought it was for the sake of the girls whose day was invariably ruined if Arithmetic was first thing in the morning. Others believed that he did it so that he could pinch some of the recess time for Arithmetic. There seems some truth in this, since his pupils were always the last to come for recess.

In place of Arithmetic, Mr Okehi has introduced Scripture as the first subject in the morning. It was a relief to most pupils. Scripture usually only involved the reading aloud of one Bible story or another. Everyone took part in the reading. The verses were read out *in sequence* until the end of the story, each pupil standing up in turn to read his verse. There was usually no caning unless an unfortunate pupil came across an unpronounceable name such as Nebuchadnezzar or Jehoshaphat. In the event of such a mishap, Mr Okehi was kind enough to allow the pupil three attempts. If he failed after that, he got the cane.

But he had other ways of making his pupils earn the cane. If the reading of the Bible story was easy, he asked very difficult questions afterwards. The class was reading stories from the Old Testament that term, but when Mr Okehi chose to be difficult he picked his questions from the New Testament. Among his pet questions were, listing the twelve disciples and naming the apostles in their order of conversion.

This was such a morning. The Bible story was easy. Joseph, the youngest son of Jacob, was sold into slavery by his jealous brothers. All the pupils knew the story by heart. Even Frederick Osisiogu, the father of the class, read his verse correctly. In the circumstances, the pupils dreaded the questions which were to fellow, but Mr Okehi started off surprisingly gently:

"What were the names of Joseph's brothers?"

"His parents?"

"What made his brothers sell him?"

It was all too easy. Then Mr Okehi warmed up with his more routine questions:

"How many ribs did Adam have?"

"How many did he sacrifice to Eve?"

"The names of the kings of Israel?"

"The number and names of the tribes of Israel?"

"Abel or Cain, who was the *villian?*"

"Esau or Jacob, who cheated the other?"

By this time, the poor pupils were *in a daze.* Not even Mark Obike, who usually remembered everything, could cope with the speed of this *volley of questions.* Mr Okehi was among them with the canes, going 'swish' with every wrong answer or blank stare. He came to Israel Nwandu. Israel was one of those lucky children who was baptised in infancy. He therefore did not have to attend the catechism classes which were compulsory for the other children in preparation for the Baptism examination.

Israel's Scripture was shaky on account of this. How he prayed for Arithmetic as Mr Okehi approached with the canes! Even the impossible H.C.F. (Highest Common Factor) and L.C.M. (Lowest Common Multiple) would have been preferable at this time. Mr Okehi knew Israel's weakness, and enjoyed tormenting the poor boy:

"Israel, now recite the Ten Commandments!" he ordered.

"Goodness gracious!" Israel thought. "Surely this man must hate me. Fancy asking the others such, simple questions, and me this..."

"Israel, the Ten Commandments, I said!" Mr Okehi repeated, interrupting Israel's thoughts.

"Sir, honour thy father and thy mother." "Is that all, Israel?"

There was no answer. Israel knew no more

"Is that all, I said?" Swish! Swish! Swish! Israel dodged and fended, but the strokes still got through.

"All right now, Israel, where do the Ten Commandments…?"

He had hardly finished the question when Israel blurted out: "Exodus Chapter 20, verse 1 to 17, Sir."

That shook Mr Okehi. He knew the chapter himself, but could not swear that he was so sure of the verses. He must look that up. He could not do any more to Israel then, but ordered: "For the twentieth time, Israel, go home and learn the Ten Commandments!"

Mr Okehi turned to continue his *rampage*. But immediately, the big hand-bell went for a change of lessons. The pupils of Standard Two were thus saved from further bruising in the name of Scripture. He returned to his table. The next subject was English. After those forty minutes of Scripture, both he and his pupil needed some rest, especially as the subject to follow was Arithmetic. Furthermore, Mr Okehi had to mark the homework before the Arithmetic lesson. What a lesson it would be if Scripture was like this!

For the English lesson he decided on a composition. He would have preferred Dictation to test their spelling, but, remembering the annoying interruptions of that fool Frederick with his: "What, Sir!", "Eh Sir?", "Again, Sir", Mr Okehi decided *to save his temper*. Frederick was so daft that he had once blurted out on hearing a difficult word at Dictation: "Spell it, Sir!" He always cupped his left hand behind his ear during Dictation. Occasionally, he had even cupped his right hand as well. No wonder he often missed out whole sentences. There was only one word to describe his atrocious spelling! Here he was in good company, with Dorcas. Dorcas Abosi was a sweet little girl who always strove to do her best, but at the announcement of Dictation she would almost *swoon*.

As Mr Okehi sat at his table he announced: "Take out your English exercise books, and write a composition of not more than two pages on the subject on the board. Write the heading before you start. Underline it. Write the date on the top right-hand corner of the page. Underline it. Leave a margin when you write, and make good paragraphs: Do not erase any word you have written down. If you want to cancel any word you do not like, do so with one straight line drawn with the help of a ruler. Cross your t's. Dot your i's but not capital I's. Spell every word correctly. Is that all clear? Off you go then!"

He whipped out the red pencil and pounced on the homework.

"But, Sir, what do we write about? I mean the subject?" someone at the back of the class. Asked, lifting an exercise book to hide his face. Mr Okehi *stifled a frown* when he realized his omission. Without saying a word, he rose, took a piece of chalk, and printed boldly on the blackboard: MY BEST FRIEND'. He sat down again, certain that no one, not even his monitor Bassey, would write about him.

The good things of life always seem to be short-lived. To the pupils of Standard Two, this seemed painfully true that morning. As the next bell went for change of lessons, it seemed only about ten minutes since the same bell had saved them from the torment of the first lesson. Now, that same bell sounded like a death knell. Arithmetic to come, with Mr Okehi fu! of energy after his rest, was a forbidding prospect. However, with some luck, that merciful bell would come to their rescue again; but then Mr Okehi did not always obey the bell when it called for recess.

When at the bell, therefore, Mr Okehi barked orders to the monitor to collect the exercise books; the pupils steeled themselves for another blistering forty minutes. The girls could not conceal their dejection and resignation. Some were beginning to dry their moist palms (moist from fear and anxiety) on their khaki skirts. Mr Okehi might be beastly, but he had the decency not to flog the girls on their buttocks or over their shoulders. He always asked them to offer one palm or the other, and the girls had learnt from bitter experience that a moist palm hurt more than a dry one or so they thought.

Bring out your Arithmetic books. We shall do the exercise you had for homework."

His routine was to deal with the homework first, calling out each pupil's mark, and promptly administering one stroke of the cane for each sum wrong as the pupil was handed back his or her exercise book. Then the new exercise for the day followed, and at the end fresh homework was set as a parting shot.

The exercise book at the top of the pile belonged to poor Dorcas, so she was called first. She stood up, looking *forlorn*. Predictably, she had got all four sums wrong. Mr Okehi announced that without any surprise. He knew that Dorcas's parents were not educated and so could not help her with her homework, and that Dorcas would not ask anyone else to do her sums for her. She just plodded on, and if she got them all wrong, that was that. He knew all that, but did not care.

As Dorcas prepared to move out of her seat and forward to the slaughter, Mr J.O.Mozie, the Standard Five teacher and Assistant Headmaster, suddenly appeared at the arched doorway, raised a hand to Mr Okehi, and walked in.

"Class up!" the monitor promptly ordered. He was well trained, this boy Bassey.

They sprang to their feet.

"Salute!"

"Good morning, *Sir*!" "Good morning everyone.

Please be seated."

After they had all sat down, Dorcas stood up again. She knew that the class teacher would not forget after the interruption.

The two teachers talked quietly, confidentially, for some time. Then Mr Okehi showed Mr Mozie the exercise to be done and also the exercise books containing the previous day's homework, and returned the exercise books to the pupils. He then asked those who had all four correct to put up their hands. He congratulated the two or three who did so. Next he asked for those with three, then two, and then one correct, making encouraging remarks to each group. Finally, he asked for the Dorcas group --those who didn't have anyone correct. They too put up their hands. Mr Mozie went on to solve the problems one after another on the blackboard, encouraging the pupils to ask questions about anything they did not understand. He gave them reasons for every step in the working out of tl answers, and asked them to correct the numbers they got wrong and to submit the corrected work to their class teacher.

After that he awakened their interest by taking them rapidly through the multiplication tables from two to twelve, even though he realized that this was too elementary. They relished it nevertheless. It gave even the dullest and the most timid among them some confidence.

When Mr Mozie came to the lesson for the day, he was so methodical and gentle about it that even Dorcas and Frederick seemed to follow what was happening. Frederick took his hand off his ear, and that was a good enough sign. He went through a few exercises with them on the board, making sure that they understood the reason for each step. He asked a few of the pupils to solve some of the problems themselves on the board. He then set one on the board for all of them to work out on their own. Almost everyone got it correct. When the hand-bell went for recess, the children would very willingly have spent more time doing Arithmetic. But Mr Mozie gave them marching orders:

"Put away your books. Tidy your desks. Run away as far as possible from the classroom and get some fresh air."

2

The Village School

Recess was a pleasant time to look forward to. So much was crammed into those thirty minutes-exchange of stories and tit-bits with pupils and friends from other classes; sharing of little bits of food with brothers, sisters and friends; plotting a few pranks, some *frisking* about and games, skipping and step-dancing by the girls. Recess was such fun that on its own it made school worth-while.

But on this day the pupils of Standard Two did not run as far away as possible from the classroom. They had two good reasons why they could not do so immediately. First they wanted to find out what merciful *providence* had taken their class teacher away from them at that most opportune moment. Also, even though the recess was meant to be a time for rest, there were so many duties to perform that half the recess was often wasted.

Dutiful Bassey had already marched off to *the fire*-wood shed where the boys on firewood duty were to show him their bundles of wood before carrying them to Mr Okehi's house. Whatever had happened to the class teacher, he, the monitor, had to do his duty. After the firewood inspection, he was to inspect the buckets of water brought by the girls.

Apart from these duties,. Bassey shared out duties to the pupils and these too had to do with the teacher's house. There was the watering of the flower garden, if this had not been done before classes; the sweeping of the back yard and disposal of refuse. The pupils did practically all Mr Okehi's housework. But this was not unusual. Nearly all the teachers used their pupils in this way. The place was like a beehive, as the pupils said. The workers were the pupils; the drones, the teachers.

The school compound was now certainly *buzzing with life*. All the classes had come out. The compound was a large, sprawling rectangle completely fenced in with a hedge which demanded frequent attention. There were three gates, the main one being the South gate from which a road led to join the main road to the market and shops, and ultimately *to* the distant railway station in the main town.

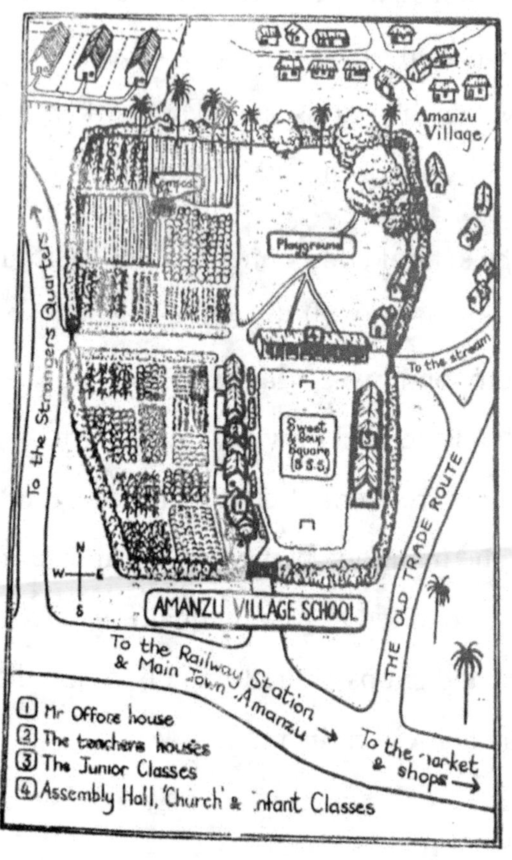

The East gate led by way of the old trade route to one of the streams in Amanzu village and also to the springs, while the West gate led to what was called the: Strangers' quarters. Here traders from other parts of the country lived.

Their main wares included textiles of local and foreign manufacture, tobacco, gunpowder, stockfish, salt, soap and kerosene. They also handled the great palm products (palm-oil and kernels) which the people of Amanzu and surrounding villages produced acting as middlemen between the villagers and the commercial houses in town. A road from this West gate also led to the Mission dispensary, which was about three miles away. There was no North gate. The school compound *abutted the* village and the hedge on the northern boundary remained unbroken. The Headmaster, Mr A.U.G. Offor, had that portion of the hedge specially fortified. This did not prevent the pupils from scaling it, nor did it stop village or even schoolboy trappers from cutting holes through it for their sling-traps. The business part of the Central School actually occupied only the bottom right quarter of the compound. The main block, running west to east in the middle, served as the Assembly Hall, and housed the Infant classes and the lower Primary classes. Church services were also held here on Sundays and during the various Christian festivals throughout the year. The block housing the higher Primary classes lay at right angles to the main block and to its right, while the teachers' quarters were a row of houses, all thatched, lying again at right-angles to the main block and to its left. Naturally Mr Offor's house, which was at the southern end of the row, was the largest. The school bell stood in the Headmaster's compound, hung from a bar between two young growing trees. Each teacher had a flower garden in front of his house, and simple as these rude mud houses were, flower gardens *lent colour* to the school compound. Among the commonest flowers were hibiscus, sunflower, marigold, allamanda, croton and roses. Whatever else the teachers did, they *took pride in* their flowers and worked their pupils hard on these gardens.

The roughly square piece of ground enclosed by the buildings served many purposes. Pupils assembled there *in formation* in their respective classes for inspection before marching in for morning prayers and classes. It was also the physical training ground and the football pitch, and other open-air activities such as sing-songs and folk dancing were held there. For the visits of important visitors, such as the Supervisor of Schools, the school assembled there. It was also the starting point for marching to Empire Day celebrations or to nearby churches for joint church services. Finally, once in a while the doctor from Umuahia might pass through Amanzu, and pupils and other people from the village would be gathered in the square to receive injections.

Mr Offor regarded that square as more or less *hallowed ground*. No *frivolities* were allowed there, and pupils were forbidden to play there during their recess. Because public caning for disgraceful conduct was always done there, someone had coined the name 'Sweet and Sour Square' (shortened to S.S.S.) for this all-purpose piece of ground.

The portion of the school compound directly behind the main block was the playground where recess was traditionally spent. In one corner of it, there were two magnificent mango trees which provided many rally things mangoes (which everyone loved), the and flies (which no one loved) during the fruiting season. They also provided beautiful shade where dances were held, tops spun, sand-pies made and sand houses built, stories told, food shared and horseplay and fights held. Even the school officially recognized these magnificent mango trees. Handwork lessons (basket-weaving, rope-making and raffia work) were held in their shade in the afternoons. Many infant classes were held there, and the older pupils were taken out there for story-telling and other lessons which did not require any writing. Nor were they the *exclusive preserve* of the school children, for the Church Elders and Women's Guild also held their not very quiet meetings under these same trees. These meetings, some of which were accompanied by eating and drinking, could not conveniently be held inside the Church hall, the house of God!

This part of the compound also contained the handwork shed for pottery and carving, adjoining firewood shed and the toilets.

A number of tall palm trees stood along the north fence. These trees no longer bore palm-fruits and were out of reach as far as getting

Palm-fronds for decorations were concerned. They were therefore not of much use to the pupils, except as elegant but *unsophisticated* models for sketching during drawing lessons. In contrast, the interest of the teachers in these palm trees went beyond the *aesthetic*. The Headmaster had arranged for one of the expert wine-tappers from the adjoining village to tap them. The wine-tapper was allowed one calabash of palm-wine as his to commission, and he delivered the rest to the Headmaster who gave out some to any of the teachers who were interested. Many were.

Half of the school compound was taken up by farms. The portion directly facing the playground was the school farm. Mr Offor ran it as any village farmer would do. He planted, or rather he made the pupils plant, a low main crop of yams. His one innovation was to make long ridges instead of the traditional mounds in

which the yams were sown. He also had a large
compost pit in the middle, and here manure was
prepared for both the farm and the teacher's
gardens. Other crops such as maize, beans,
okro, pepper, vegetables and tomatoes were also
cultivated. All the pupils worked on this con
farm at various jobs according to their age and
ability.

The road to the West gate separated
this school farm from the gardens behind the
teachers' quarters. Each teacher had his back
'garden'. The teachers grew maize, beans,
tomatoes, onions, gourds, cucumber, pepper,
other green vegetables, and anything apart from
yams or cassava. By the Headmaster's crafty
definition only yams or cassava would make
these 'gardens' qualify as farms. So to keep
them and be able to present them to the
Supervisor of Schools and other visitors as
'garden', yams and cassava were *tabooed*. Who

worked on these 'gardens'? The 'worker bees' of course.

3

School and Marriage

Abigail Onuoha was one of the most relieved pupils in the class at the sudden disappearance of Mr Okehi, their class teacher. She hated Arithmetic the way Mr Okehi taught it. Abigail was a neat, pretty little girl of about nine years. She was *chubby* with a round amiable face, with large eyes *accentuated* by long eyelashes. Her skin was smooth and dark, her hair jet black, close-cropped as the school ordered, and parted on the right.

Girls below Standard Five were forbidden to plait their hair. The school regulation was that their hair must be cut short and, if parted, must be parted on the right. The boys were to part their hair on the left. No one was allowed to part his or her hair in the middle. This was regarded as a sign of overconfidence. In fact it had been recognized as such in local usage, the hairstyle with parting in the middle being called: 'I don't care' which had *evolved* into 'Adonkia' in the local parlance.

Abigail's father was quite rich *by local standards*. He was an ivory merchant from Abiriba, living and working there in Amanzu. Abigail's two brothers in their teens had already taken to their father's trade and were already trudging the roads to Bende, Umuahia and Aba selling their precious wares. At that time, many people considered it a waste of their sons' time, to keep them in school beyond the addition and subtraction stage of the Arithmetic lessons. Oddly enough a few people did not mind letting their daughters stay on a little longer until they were big enough to marry. So Abigail's prospects were quite bright, even though she started school rather late. Furthermore, Abigail's mother, who had become an active and influential member of the Church Women's Guild, had decided that all her remaining children should have as much education as possible. She was not going to let Abigail's father take them out of school. Already she had put little Johnny, who was not yet five, into school. She calculated that she should really have had five children in that school instead of two, but the one born between the two big boys and Abigail, and two more between Abigail and little Johnny, had all died young. She would still do it, she promised herself. Since little Johnny, two more had been born and by the help of God, there might be others to follow.

Abigail had shown Bassey her water and carried it to Mr Okehi's house. She returned her bucket to the shed, brushed some sand and drops of water off her brown Khaki skirt, and washed her hands. That was the school uniform for girls -brown khaki skirts and white blouses which were more like tunics. One small pocket was allowed on the blouse and one on the skirt. Even though it was Friday, Abigail's uniform was still very neat. Her friends said she was lucky that one of her father's tenants was a washerman. Therefore, Abigail was outstandingly neat and tidy.

She was heading for the sand-pit in the playground to look for little Johnny when someone hailed her: "There you are, Abbie! Little Johnny's been crying for you." Abigail turned. The speaker was Miss Chima, with little Johnny *in tow.*

"Yes, Miss," Abigail answered and ran to meet them.

Miss Chima was the only full-time lady teacher in the Central School. The only other lady who taught at the school was the Catechist's wife, Mrs Sabina Imo, a kindly middle-aged matron of *ample* proportions who took the bigger girls in needlework and sewing. Mrs Imo had a number of girls engaged to be married, who came to live with her for some months before their marriage. This 'brushing up', as it was called, had *superseded* the older custom of 'going into the flattening-room' before marriage. It had become the fashionable thing for young parishioners who could afford it to send their be*trothed* to be 'brushed up' by educated and prominent ladies such as Pastors' wives, Catechist' wives or Headmasters' wives. These ladies taught their wards housekeeping, cookery, sewing and needlework, social *etiquette*, and, in some cases, to read the Bible. Mrs Imo often brought some of these young women to the school to do needlework with the bigger girls.

It was not usual to have full-time lady teachers in the Central School, Amanzu, and the circumstances of Miss Chima's appointment were quite *unique*. The Mission had started an experiment, about six years ago, by building a boarding Primary School for girls. This school was built on a beautiful site on a hill in a town called Ama-Oji. It bore the grand name of Girl's Demonstration School, Mission Hill, Ama-Oji. The first Headmistress was Miss J. Hill, a reputedly very talented educationist and university graduate who came from England.

It was proposed to have classes from Standard One to Standard Six, and to prepare the students for secondary school education or for teacher training or other professional courses such as nursing. At that time there were only two secondary schools for girls in the country, and both of them were in Lagos.

Miss Hill did not want to start with one *solitary* class and take six whole years to build up, nor did she want to take in students who would not stay long enough to benefit from the new system. She therefore *struck* a *mean,* and started with three classes: Standards One, Two and Three. This involved combing all the Primary Schools around for suitable girls in those classes. Girls were selected from as far afield as Calabar, Port Harcourt, Onitsha and Enugu.

The Girl's Demonstration School scheme was an immediate success. The training was so good that soon the girls from there stood *out a mile* from girls from other schools. They grew faster, looked fitter and prettier and were more courteous, spoke better, and carried themselves much better. But in this excellence lay the danger to the school.

By the time the first two sets had passed Standard Six and left the school, young men could no longer wait for the girls to pass Standard Six. They were beginning to marry the girls still in school, first the bigger ones, then the younger ones. For the younger ones, they offered their parents *irresistible* deposits or a hand with the school fees. That was not as odd as it might sound. After all, it was not so long ago when deposits were paid on baby girls within the first few weeks of their birth, and such *covenants* were never broken nor were the subsequent marriages any less successful than those contracted between adults.

Nothing could deter these desperate young men from carrying off the girls in school. Bride prices *rocketed*, but they got the money somehow. Miss Hill pleaded with the p of her girls, but many argued that the sole purpose of educating the girls was to get them married off profitably and happily. How then could they be expected to resist these young men with money and secure jobs? Why, some of these young men actually owned motor-bikes and others boasted they could buy motor-cars.

Poor Miss Hill, what could she do? She reported to the Manager, the Reverend William Jones, who lived in Port Harcourt. It gave her a severe jolt to learn that he did not seem to share her distress. Perhaps he had been in West Africa so long that he was beginning to feel and to think like the parents of those girls. He even dared to suggest (whether in jest or seriously, she was not sure) that she might do well to increase her intake of students. The utter *absurdity*! Was she there to run a wife-making factory for these half-educated men, or to demonstrate how girls should be educated? She wondered whether she should give up the mad venture and return home to England. But she was determined to *press on.* She remembered her Yorkshire background. The daughter of a Yorkshire man must not give in. She returned to her school, to her girls, determined *to fight to the finish.*

At Christmas that year she was still *depressed* by the same problem and wrote a long letter to the Manager, extracts from which included: ".... That is what is with our Protestant Church, too much individual freedom ... We are not the first to build a residential school *for* girls in this area

The Roman Catholics have been running Convents around here for years... They do not allow any nonsense in their Convents, and the girls go through their full training. If this sort of marriage-fever had started in their Convents, they would probably have the parents of these girls *brought* to *book*. But here, because we want to encourage these people to come to Church, we allow them to maintain some of their bad old customs Christianity was never easy. It should not be made easy for people just to get them in ..... Child marriage is a form of slavery. It is *savage.* It is unChristian.... Did William Wilberforce, Abraham Lincoln, Bishop Crowther and other brave Christian fighters against the slave trade and slavery give their lives so that Christianity would come here to *connive* at these same sins *in miniature*?... If nothing can be done about this intolerable situation I shall have no alternative but to resign and return to my native Yorkshire....."

At the beginning of the following term, early in January, a worse situation awaited them. Only five girls in Standard Six and eight in Standard Five returned to the Girl's Demonstration School, and this, out of classes that ought to be about thirty. It had been like an *epidemic.* Christmas was always the worst season. Even the lower classes did not escape. There were barely enough girls to constitute Standard Four. Miss Pitts, Miss Hill's deputy, was in tears. She moaned that that sort of thing never happened in Lagos. There the parents were intelligent, and the girls *ambitious*, not so kitchen-crazy. The young men had a choice, a very wide choice. There were the two secondary schools; there were the working girls; there were even girls educated in England.

Miss Hill's state was indescribable. She made another painful journey to Port Harcourt. Reverend William Jones had received her letter. He looked visibly disturbed this time. But he would still not urge any rash or harsh measures, as these might have the effect of discouraging the parents who were obviously enthusiastic about having their daughters properly educated.

"Properly educated, *Mr* Jones!" Miss Hill broke in, unable to help herself. Then she apologized.

The Manager appreciated her distress. He assured her that things would work out all right in the end if they all maintained their faith in the Almighty. He told her of his more painful experiences fifteen to twenty years before. Then he told her that the Mission Education Council had been summoned to decide what further steps should be taken. She was to close down Standards Five and Six, distribute the few students left in those classes among nearby schools and promote a few of the best girls from Standard Three to make Standard Four up to a respectable size. Two of the junior teachers would have to be transferred.

Miss Hill was very sore about the breakup of her school, especially about the loss of her senior pupils. She said it was *ironic* that these poor girls should have to suffer the indignity of being sent down to mixed schools because their thoughtless classmates had run off to marry from school. But Reverend Jones explained patiently that the Mission could not afford to run classes of five and eight pupils or to I maintain redundant teachers, and he strove to reassure Miss Hill that she would live to see her school back to its old glory before long. Miss Hill's Girl's Demonstration School was practically back to where it had started.

So it was Miss Comfort Chima, who had passed her Standard Six in the Central School, Amanzu, and had taken a two-year Teacher Training course at Oron before going to teach in the Girl's Demonstration *the* School, found herself once more in the Central School Amanzu. She assisted the Church teacher, Mr Obiako, in taking the infant classes. With her came two girls, one in Standard Six and the other in Standard Five, who were among the lucky ones to be sent down from Mission Hill.

49

4

Miss Chima's Children

Miss Chima had grown fond of Abigail because she was so neat and well behaved, looking very much like some of the girls she had taught at the Girl's Demonstration School. She hoped to get Abigail into that school, and had already mentioned her in a letter to Miss Hill. Abigail's class teacher had told Miss Chima that Abigail was dull and that, as her parents were not educated, they could not help her at home. Miss Chima resolved *to coach* Abigail on her own.

When Abigail joined Miss Chima and little Johnny, he told her at once how 'Miss' had taken him to her house and given him biscuits.

There was ample evidence of this around his mouth, on his clothes and in his hands.

Miss Chima *and her "School Children."*

"Thank you very much, Miss," Abigail said. "Oh, that's nothing to thank me for, Abbie. Then Abigail asked little Johnny whether he had thanked 'Miss'. "Miss, thank you," he promptly said.

Abigail opened the parcel of food which their mother had wrapped for them. It was boiled yam thoroughly soaked in red palm oil and flavoured with pepper and salt. She took out one wedge-shaped piece and gave it to little Johnny. He grabbed it with both hands, dropping the piece of biscuit he still had, and was pushing the whole piece into his mouth at once, when Abigail pulled him up and said: "Don't eat like a pig, Johnny."

Miss Chima laughed and asked Abigail if she was not going to have any of the yam.

"No, Miss," she answered, "we ate before coming to school in the morning."

They walked towards the sand-pit, past groups of children skipping or clap-dancing or *twirling* tops. Johnny pressed on with his mid-morning meal. Miss Chima knew that she had left some water at the sand-pit, so little Johnny could have a drink when he got through his second mid-morning *guzzle*.

As they passed two of Abigail's classmates, Mary and Adanma, who were skipping, Mary called out to Abigail: "Abbie, ask Miss if she knows where our teacher is."

Abigail had actually thought of asking

Miss Chima about their teacher's mysterious disappearance, but she did not know how to put it.

As they walked on, Miss Chima asked: "What is this about your teacher?? By The way, why don't you join your friends there? I'll take little Johnny to the sand-pit to join the other children. Your recess will soon be over, and you have not enjoyed yourself."

"My uniform will get dirty, Miss."

"Ah! No, no, no! you must play games, Abbie! Miss Hill won't like you *one little bit* if you don't. She is very fond of games, and of girls who are good at games."

"Yes, Miss, I like games. I like the ones we play after school when we take off our school uniforms and play in our *chemises*. I also like to drill and run. I skip at home, and can skip better than Mary and Adanma. They know it. It's only that I don't like to be around when I am wearing the school uniform."

In that case, Abbie, you will be quite happy if you go to Mission Hill. There everyone has a separate dress for games."

Little Johnny was taking no further part in the conversation. "Miss, thank you," had been his last contribution. He was too preoccupied with eating, nay wolfing his oil-soaked and pepper-flavoured meal. As one piece of yam after another disappeared into his overworked little mouth, all he did was stretch out a hand to Abigail for the next piece as if to say with princely discourtesy: "Next, waitress!"

They eventually arrived at the sand-pit. It was crowded. Two little boys in brown knee-length tunics (the school uniform for the infant classes) were throwing sand into each other's eyes. Their aim was so poor that none of their excited spectators escaped. What could children of four and five find to fight about? Perhaps a piece of stick to play with, or a sand-house built by one of them, or even just an unmarked seat in the sandpit? "Funny little things," Miss Chima thought.

As the dusty spectators saw her, some raised the alarm: "Miss is coming! Miss is coming!" Then they proceeded to give their varied versions of the cause of the fight, and to pronounce their divided verdicts. Amidst the chatter, no one could hear anything.

Meanwhile, the tough little *combatants* had disengaged and were rubbing their eyes. Their hands, faces, bodies, tunics and the sand-pit were all one dusty brown. What they needed most urgently was a bath, not a verdict.

Just then, the big hand-bell rang for the end of recess. The boy responsible for the hand-bell that week was Reuben Madu, of the big muscular boys in Standard Six. He ought to have been in the Police Force, not in school. When he started swinging the bell around with both hands, it sounded like an unbroken *sequence* of deafening thunder bolts.

Abigail curtsied to Miss Chima (one of the tips she had learnt from Miss about life at the Mission Hill) and ran back towards the classroom, leaving 'Miss' to sort out little

Johnny and the crowd in the sand-pit. Good luck to her! On the way, she remembered that she had not after all told Miss Chima about their teacher. She could not go back to her now. She ran on.

The morning session was over at noon. For the Infant class, school was now over for the day. All the other classes returned at two for the afternoon session. Miss Chim had to ensure the safe conduct of her pupils to their homes. For those like little Johnny, who had older sisters or brothers in the school, it was easy. She handed them over to these older children. Some mothers who lived in the nearby village or in the Stranger's Quarters came for their children. But she still had some whom she personally took back to their homes on the way to the market, and others whom she took all the way to their mothers in the market.

This was the daily market which was about one and a half miles away and quite near the shops, with the Railway Station a little farther on. In this market the women sold various foodstuffs, including gari, cassava, yams, vegetables, oranges, bananas, groundnuts and a hundred and one other little things.

Miss Chima enjoyed these visits to the market. The mothers of the children were grateful and other market women were always *thrilled* to see her. She had become quite an important person, the first full time lady teacher. She had grown up in Amanzu, but now that her father had been promoted to Grade 1 District interpreter and had been transferred to the District Headquarters in Bende, she lived with Mr Offor the Headmaster, who was a very good man, a friend of her family, and married. Mr and Mrs Offor were fond of her. The only thing she did not like was that even Mrs Offor, who was her mother's friend and had called her Com (short for Comfort) when she was a pupil in the same school, had joined all the other people in *the universal custom* of calling her 'Miss'. It was so personal. It was considered a mark of respect for her *elevated* status. She was almost forgetting that she had a name. It had not been so bad at Mission Hill. The students were taught to address the teachers as Miss A or Miss B, but not Miss Nothing. She was Miss Chima, alright. Of course her fellow teachers all called her by her pet name: Com., Even Miss Pitts (though never Miss Hill) had learnt to call her this, even though she made it sound like 'come'. Miss Pitts could never get that sleepy, beautiful local *inflexion* which prolonged both the 'o' and the 'm'.

The merciless mid-day sun beat the ground with fury through a clear cloudless sky. Even for the walk of one and a half miles to the market, Miss Chima had to prepare against the sun. She went home to change her footwear from the tightly laced white canvas shoes, which the Headmaster had decreed for all the teachers, *to* the more airy leather sandals which she had worn in her old school. She folded a thin, floral silk scarf into a triangle and put it over her head, knotting it loosely under her chin, and pulling the front well forward over her forehead, almost like a veil, to keep out the *glare* of the sun. She had an umbrella, but did not believe in using it against the sun. She thought that should be left to older women. Besides, it could be an *encumbrance*. She needed both hands free to hold her children. In fact at the beginning of her round, some of the children could count themselves lucky if they could cling to one finger. Others tugged at her skirt and it was a job to walk, anchored as she was on all sides. She must at times have looked like the Pied Piper of Hamelin.

When she was ready she collected the children, and they set off. They left the school premises by the South gate and crossed the main road to walk on the left side of the road. The crossing was quite leisurely and unhurried. There was no danger of being run over by a car. Very few cars passed through this old trade route. Once in a while the doctor's car did, but if this was to happen, notices would have been given in the Church and school weeks ahead. The transport lorries carrying palm-kernels and palm oil from neighbouring towns to the commercial houses usually stopped in the main town. Occasionally one of these lorries would be hired to clear a large *consignment* of palm produce from Amanzu Village. This was such a rare event that it was bound to be known about beforehand.

The real danger on this road was the bicycle, not the car. Cyclists were so arrogant and so *delirious* with their new-found power and importance that the mad young ones among them sometimes zig-zagged across the road, chasing and frightening 'poor and lowly' pedestrians out of their wits. Mercifully, however, these bicycle riders also enjoyed hearing the sound of their own bicycle bells so much that the pedestrian always had ample warning of their approach. These were also the days of the loud hand-pumped motor car horns. Some cyclists bought these horns and fitted them to their bicycles in place of, or more commonly in addition to, their bicycle bells. The noise which was made by alternately or *simultaneously* ringing the bell and sounding the horn was *weird*, but how these cyclists enjoyed it!

Miss Chima and her children were keeping to the cooler, grass-covered side of the road. The sandy middle of the road was too hot to walk on. The shade offered by the overhanging branches and boughs also helped to keep the side of the road cooler. Some children loved skipping from one tuft of cool grass to the other in order to avoid walking on the hotter sandier patches. Miss Chima was being dragged about from one conversation to the other, and tried good naturedly to keep up with all.

As they were coming down the first *incline,* the inevitable alarm of an approaching cyclist rang out from behind them with its customary loudness and persistence. It alarmed no one. All the children were used to it. They clung closer to Miss Chima merely out of habit. Scarcely any of them turned to see who was coming.

Suddenly, someone raised the cry: "London Boy!" The other children echoed: "London Boy! London Boy!" and all turned to see if it was really 'London Boy' on the bicycle. 'London Boy' was not a boy at all, but a dandy, *jocund* and rather flippant man in his thirties who had never been anywhere near London in his life. He was the popular tailor in town, and made school uniforms for the Central School, St Luke's School, and some smaller schools in the area. His other nicknames were: 'Golden Boy' and: 'Sea-Never Dry', both of which stemmed from his immodest claims to affluence. His undoubted extravagance showed that money passed through his hands but not proof that he was rich.

He was a trick cyclist, and owed his popularity more to this than to his *sartorial* efficiency. In fact, he was too careless and too juvenile in outlook to be a good tailor. The children adored him because one of his tricks was hoisting as many as ten of them on various parts of his bicycle and on his person as he demonstrated his *prowess*. His bicycle was bedecked with bicycle licenses of the past dozen years or so and with tiny flags and medals which he claimed to have won in bicycles races in Port Harcourt and Aba in his younger days. As this man bluffed his way through life with one nickname or another, few cared for his real name Philemon Wagbara. He came from Aba, and was quiet, Philemon a good man at heart.

As the children looked up the hill, the bicycle rider appeared on the crest and was steaming down at full speed towards them. But alas! He was not a 'London Boy'. "Oh, it is the Standard Three teacher," one of them sighed.

Then another one shouted with more enthusiasm: "It is the Standard Three teacher!" and this was followed by calls of "Carry me, Sir!" by several children all begging for a lift. Begging *or* commanding? Well that was their language. They meant no discourtesy, but it was too long-winded to shout: "Please carry me, Sir". Besides, 'Sir' made up for everything. It had a built-in overtone of courtesy and humility.

Mr B. M. Agomuo, the Standard Three teacher, was no trickster. He could not compete with 'London Boy' the tailor. In fact he was not even a competent rider yet, having bought his bicycle only recently, a great event which had called for a celebration. He therefore approached Miss Chima and her lively group of little children with unconcealed caution. He helped the weak brakes of his second-hand bicycle by dragging his left foot along the ground, off and on, as he got near them. Then, steadying his bicycle tremulously with his right hand, he swooped clumsily, picked up one of the little girls in the group, and slung her incompetently astride his bicycle. That was really poor cyclemanship, sitting a little girl *astride* a bicycle frame instead of sitting her sideways. But Mr Agomuo was a cycling novice. He was glad not to have fallen off his perch, and while some of the other children ran after him still shrieking: "Carry me, Sir!," he waved hesitantly to the group, wobbled a little across the sandy road, and rode away hailing over his shoulder: "Be coming, Chaps!"

He was obviously heading for the market and was sure to hand little Monica over to her mother at her stall where she sold silk kerchief, coloured beads, bangles, necklaces and rings. She would probably buy Mr Agomuo some fruit. But oh, what a rare sight!

5

Friday Afternoon

The afternoon *session* on Friday was in effect a work session, and little besides. But some clever man, probably Mr Offor, the Headmaster, or possibly the one before him, had *contrived* to sandwich this unpopular work session between two other activities from which the pupils could not escape. The first was the weekly General Knowledge test which preceded the manual work, and the other was the singing lessons in preparation for the compulsory Sunday church services. The singing followed the manual work, and then finally the weekly House matches were played football for the boys and volley-ball for the girls.

Since the marks for the General Knowledge tests were added up at the end of the term, these tests ensured that all the pupils turned up for the afternoon sessions. The *vigilance* of the class monitors and the teachers could be relied on to prevent pupils from slipping away after the tests until the work was done. Then there were inter-house matches to play or to watch. With only two houses, 'A' and 'B' as they were called, the bitterness between them, particularly in football, almost approached the venom of inter school ties. More *brawling* developed between the spectators than between the players; and whereas the referee's whistle could bring the end of hostilities on the field, its effect on the spectators was often the opposite.

The sun was still *hammering down* on the parched school Assembly Square ("The Sweet and Sour Square") when the second bell went for the afternoon session. It was two o'clock.

The pupils fell into line in their classes, stamping about restlessly because of the intense heat of the ground under their unshoed feet. A teacher was posted at the main gate, the south gate, with a bundle of canes in one hand. Swish, swish! he meted out to every latecomer as he or she scampered past. The Assistant Headmaster, Mr Mozie, who took these afternoon assemblies, usually made them snappy. As soon as the classes had fallen into straight lines, he marched them in, leaving the stragglers to the mercy of the teacher at the gate or of their class teachers.

These weekly General Knowledge tests were accorded *all the dignity of* real examinations, complete with such trimmings, as unfamiliar invigilators who, with hawk-like watchfulness, prevented *cribbing* or any form of cheating. Mr Agomuo, the Standard Three teacher, came in to supervise Standard Two.

The prim and proper Bassey gave him the standard reception: "Class up!... Salute!.. b. Class sit!" Mr Agomuo looked *full of confidence*, or rather, full of himself. He was standing feet apart, his hands thrust deep into his pockets. His *curt* "Afternoon" in response to their full throated: "Good afternoon, Sir!" had a note of disdain in it. It was in his nature, and the nickname 'Big Mouth', which the school child n had coined from his initials 'B.M', suited him well. If they had seen him in a less dignified stance on his bicycle a few hours before; he might have qualified for another nickname, the pupils' only way of having their own back on the teachers.

Mr Agomuo copied out on the board the General Knowledge questions he had collected from the Headmaster's office, and then announced: "Thirty minutes, chaps!" The term 'chaps' was one of the slang words which Mr

Agomuo had picked up on his football rounds, and he threw it about carelessly. *If* the Headmaster caught him using slang in class, he would be in trouble. Mr Offor was *dead against* slang and Pidgin English in class.

Mr Agomuo was a bad teacher. Like his friend, Mr Okehi, he believed very much in the magic powers of the cane. Having set down the questions on the board, he picked up some of the remaining canes which had been rearranged on the table by the monitor after Mr Okehi's morning rampage. He then took measured paces up and down the class, sniffing the air *maliciously* for any misbehaviour that would call for the cane. But he had no luck. Apart from old Frederick who had his cocked left hand more or less permanently behind his ear as if listening for inspiration, a few muffled groans and sighs here and there and *squinting* by some of the pupils in the corners on the back rows,

Mr Agomuo could not fault this class on any count. Even the girls looked in no trouble at all. It was as if the entire class had conspired to deny him the fun of using his cane.

The minutes passed. Bored, Mr Agomuo returned to the table. He heard the crack of a cane from an adjacent classroom swish! swish!, and pricked his ears to find out where it was coming from. "Lucky man," he probably thought.

Then his mind returned to the more profitable subject of football. That was one thing he was good at, and he loved the game. He was big and strong, played left back or centre half for the Wanderers' team in town, and boasted about it. His nickname fitted both his character and his build. The Wanderers Club was formed by a group of young traders in town and Mr Agomuo told *grandiose* stories about the origin of the name. He was due to play for them again the following day against a rival traders' team, and was making mental schemes of the match when the hand-bell interrupted him.

He got up and ordered rather absentmindedly: "Monitor, collect the papers!" Then he stood aside to look at the questions on the board as if to accuse the questions of joining in the plot to make the pupils not earn the cane. But the questions were not simple. They covered the usual range of the subject - Geography, historical names and dates, the. stations on the newly-built railway, the seasons, crops, animals and flowers. He was still peering at the board when Mr Okehi walked in through the doorway. The startled class scrambled to their feet and saluted. Mr Agomuo greeted him: "Hello, D.S., are you back?"

Yes, thanks it's terrible, **B.M.**how goes it?" Mr Okehi replied.

The teachers usually addressed one another by their initials, a practice exploited by the pupils in coining nicknames. The one *disparaging* that most of the time it was referred to only in the initials in which it was concealed, D.S.'. He looked particularly deserving of the name this afternoon. He was *drenched* with sweat, his shirt stuck to his body. His close cropped hair was in knots, and his face grimy and studded with beads of sweat. Like the little fighters in the sandpit earlier on, what he needed was a wash, not a *verdict* on his class.

"You have a wonderful class, D.S.," Mr Agomuo observed *cynically*, still bristling with annoyance.

"Not in your life! What, wonderful? Impossible. Not this wretched lot. Wait until I have taken them in Arithmetic," Mr Okehi disagreed. Then he turned to his monitor: "Eh, by the way, Bassey, what happened about the Arithmetic this morning?" Then, "Dorcas..."

"I must be off now, D.S., before my lazy boys all *melt away*." Mr Agomuo stopped Mr Okehi from his pounce on Dorcas.

"That's right, B.M. Thanks a lot. I'll give you the full story when I have organised some work for these idlers."

Mr Agomuo left, dying to learn about Mr Okehi's dash from the school in the morning, and wondering what he meant when he said: "It's terrible".

Mr Okehi always had the measure of his class. Organizing time for work was not difficult.

"Abigail, Dorcas and the order girls, and you, you and you good-for-nothings in front, go to the stream and fetch water," he started.

"Yes, Sir."

"Frederick, Abel, Israel, Olatunji and Shadrach to the fence!"

"Yes, Sir."

"The rest, carry out the benches and desks; sweep the classroom; wash the benches and desks; bring back the desks here and carry the benches to the Church Hall."

"Yes, Sir."

"Monitor, you know your work blackboard and easel to the vestry; tables and chairs to my house after they have been washed; keep an eye on everybody."

"Yes, Sir."

"All clear to everyone?"

"Yes, Sir-r-r-r-r!"

"Off you go then!"

6

Rumours Fly

The air was *thick with rumours*. Throughout the village and in the town there were varying reasons. The Headmaster was going! No one knew for certain how or where the rumour started, but once out, spreading it was no difficulty. Amanzu was a small community, practically a closed one. The main *component* parts of it, the village in which the Central School stood, the Strangers' Quarters, and the main town or 'the beach' were all close together. For a little inland place about a hundred miles from the sea, and nowhere near a lake, the main town of Amanzu had the unlikely name of 'the beach'; a name *of very recent origin* given because 'the beach' like the river and the seaports, handled all the palm-produce trade through the middlemen and the commercial houses. There was no newspaper. But from the way stories flew around, there seemed to have been an unwritten understanding that any story, rumour or gossip which started should be passed on 'without much delay'. However there was no clause reading 'without much alteration'.

The rumour had been heard first in the town, not in the school. Mr Okehi's summons by the Headmaster and his dash from the important *errand* started its own spate of *conjectures* about him in the school. Mr Okehi's Standard Two pupils, who were far from fond of him, were responsible for the inspired guesses started during the recess that he was going on transfer or that he was going to be *demoted* because he had failed the Pupil

Teachers' second year examination for the second time. Someone even suggested that he was going to be sacked altogether. Frederick's (hand behind the ear) version was that Mr Okehi was going to join the Police Force so that he could flog people as he pleased. There were other suggestions. No one knew which, if any, was correct.

Mr Okehi's reappearance in the afternoon did not immediately settle the issues. The comment he made to Mr Agomuo: "It's terrible", was non-committal. Perhaps it supported the story of his going. "How marvellous!" some of his pupils thought.

When the pupils hit the village and the town with their own *theories* about Friday's happenings in the school, the result was confusion. To the original rumour with which the people had been *grappling* for about a week, that of the Headmaster's transfer, the addition of the new rumour straight from the school itself that another teacher was also on the way out, was bound to make some people *dizzy*. It was puzzling. What was the Central School, Amanzu coming to? Closure or reduction to a Group School?

On Saturday morning, Timothy and Jonas, both members of the Committee of the Church Elders and both with children in the school, discussed the matter on their way to the market.

"What worries me is this," Jonas said. "What are we going to do about it all? The school will fall if the Headmaster goes."

"But how do we know it is true?" his friend asked.

"Know it is true? Why not? Someone didn't just slap his side and start the story, did he?" "Well, I don't know, Jonas. It's March, you know. Headmasters are not usually transferred

in March, only at the beginning of the year or at
the end."

Members of the Church Committee discussing *the truth*
of *the* rumours

"You are right, Timothy. Perhaps the story
the children brought home about the transfer of

the junior teacher is the true one. It must be true, Oh, that's much better. Let that one go. I say let him go." the *voluble* Jonas opined.

"We don't even know that that one is true unless we find out," Timothy cautioned.

"Oh, it must be true, Timothy. Let's ask the H.M. tomorrow after church service. The boys said that they saw Mr Okehi riding to Umuahia to see the Inspector."

What Inspector are you *jabbering* about now, Jonas? Inspector of Police? What for?"

"Oh, no, not the Police Inspector, but the Inspector of Schools," Jonas answered.

"Ha! Ha! Ha! Ha! Ha-a-h! Mr Dewar you mean? Is that what you call him now? Inspector? Ha! Ha!..."

"What do they call him?" Jonas broke in, irritated by the friends' laughter.

"Supervisor of Schools, man, not Inspectors of Police," Timothy corrected.

"But I didn't say Inspector of Police. Anyway, what's the big difference between Inspectors and Supervisor? The person I mean *is* the big bearded European who rides a motor-cycle. He has red hair. That's the one the children said Mr Okehi went to see."

"All right, Jonas. The children may be wrong or they may be right. Tomorrow at church, let us ask Matthew to call a committee meeting. We shall then know how to approach the H.M. on the matter."

7

Saturday Hunters

Meanwhile, for the pupils, Saturday was 'business as usual'. But it was not school business. They were individuals once more, free to follow their pet *hobbies,* free of school bells, free of monitors, free of teachers. There was fun to be had, but it was never all fun. Village life was a *veritable* mixture of fun and fending-fending for oneself, fending for one's family. Perhaps for the children from the Strangers' Quarters or from the beach there was more fun than fending. But for those from the village, the reverse was probably true.

Aaron and Ishmael Kanu lived in the village. Their family was a *polygamous* one, and accordingly large. For them, Saturday dawned particularly early because they had so many activities to cram into it. They woke up at *the* first *cock-crow* and, led by their cousin, Micah, who was about fourteen years old, they set out for the stream. Two other cousins had slept with them that night so that they could all set out together. The stream where they had laid their fish-lines the previous evening was quite a distance from their home, and they aimed to get the before the second cock-crow. They carried matchets and fly-whisks, the latter for clearing cobwebs and dew from their path. No one minded the early rising as long as it was for this fishing *adventure*. They boys were thrilled.

They walked *in single file* through the bush path, the person *to bear the brunt of* the cobwebs and dewdrops for the day having been chosen beforehand *on a rota basis*. They arrived at the stream as they planned just as the cocks were stirring again and crowing for the second time. The light was now good enough (for their trained eyes) to walk along the banks of the stream examining their lines. The number of cobwebs they had cleared on the way indicated that they were the first arrivals that morning. That was exactly what they had hoped for. Apart from wanting to get back early for other work at home, one reason why they set out so was to *forestall* some of their mischievous rivals from other villages, who often stole the early fish from their lines, or cut their lines out of jealousy or sheer wickedness.

It was remarkable how everyone remembered exactly where all his lines were laid. A clever boy like Ishmael often had up to fifteen or twenty lines. He was remarkably good at fishing even though he was not the oldest boy in the group. He had an uncanny sense of fish-rich nooks and corners, and almost always caught more fish than anyone else. Even when he laid some of his hooks in apparently open and shallow areas, he still caught fish. No wonder his cousins called him the 'fish-magnet'. He seemed to draw them to himself, or rather, to his hooks.

By about half past seven they had finished examining their lines and taking them out, fish or no fish. One disappointed boy who did not catch any fish, but still had some worms left over in his cigarette-tin container, threaded them on his hooks to have another try. The young master-fisherman, Ishmael, reminded him that it was silly to do so as the swarming shoals of very small fish were sure to pick the hook clean of worms within minutes of their being laid.

"Day fishing is *a different kettle of fish from night fishing*," he concluded with an air of quiet confidence.

Some of the boys washed their faces and feet in the stream, while one braved the cold water and had a quick dip. They set out for home. But returning home then was not for Ishmael, the little master. His hunting *instincts* were keener than most other boys. He handed over his fish and lines to his brother Aaron, and set out with their cousin Micah to inspect their traps.

Ishmael and Micah took their trapping seriously, and were *adept* at the various methods. Ishmael, though the younger of the two, was more successful or, as the boys put it, more liked by animals, which made them get caught more readily in his traps. Perhaps Ishmael owed his skill to his father, an eminent hunter who had earned the *coveted* title of 'Leopard Killer', a title which was never easy to come by. Many men died chasing that title. Ishmael looked more and more and more like his father every day. To him, schooling was merely something to while away time until he was big enough to handle a gun. Ishmael was sure about that. As far as he was concerned, Aaron and his type could go on and become teachers or clerks or whatever they liked; he couldn't care less. Aaron, two years younger, had already caught up with Ishmael at school, but so what?

"Where do we start today, Mike?" Ishmael asked as they headed into the bush.

"Well, the ground-traps first for me any day," Micah replied. "You know those crafty rabbits and hedgehogs, if they get caught, can always *wriggle* free by breaking a leg and hopping away on three, unless we get to them early. So let's go for those first.'

Ishmael knew that his cousin was right. They each cut a sizable length of stick for *a probe,* and began tracing the tracks. Laying traps was fun but it was risky too. They had to study the natural tracks of these animals and set the traps by burying them underneath suitable sections of the tracks. Sometimes they had tc make artificial tracks to resemble the natural animal tracks, However, knowing that these animals could also frisk about outside their tracks, especially when they were in company, traps could be laid at some distance from these tracks. The danger lay in forgetting where other trappers laid theirs. Trapping was popular, and the bush near the farmlands was *studded* with traps. Ishmael and Micah had consequently to tread with care, probing and poking with their sticks at suspicious sites.

They walked on. They knew where their own traps were, and gave them numbers, sometimes even names. Particularly successful traps were given pet names. They passed one, which had been partly exposed, the sand and leaves and twigs having been blown away by the wind. In that state not even the most foolish animal, unless it was also blind, would step on it. So Micah suggested that they should cover it up properly again.

"But the wind will only uncover it again,' Ishmael argued. "Why don't we dig it up and reset it instead?'

"No, Ishie, digging the moist morning soil always makes a trap look very obvious. These animals have got eyes you know. They may like you, as we say, but they won't walk into an open grave for you with their eyes wide open. I think we had better dig it up altogether, and re-lay it in the evening.

"All right, Mike, I'll take it out,' Ishmael agreed. He cut another long piece of stick off a nearby bush and trimmed it. He walked back to the trap, and with one end of the stick made a few prods along the track towards the bared trap *to stimulate* the trail of an animal.

'Snap! ... Clanger!... Clang!!' The trap went as Ishmael's stick dislodged the catch. Sand and leaves were thrown up into the air as the trap leapt out of the ground. This tickled and thrilled Ishmael, he wished it had been a real animal. As he bent down to take the trap by its chain, he heard Micah who had gone ahead call out: "Ishie, Ishie, number three has a visitor.'

Ishmael left the trap and dashed off towards his cousin shouting: "Where? Where?' Then he remembered that, in his haste, he had not picked up his matchet. He ran back to fetch it, and as he started again towards Micah, he heard him groan: "Oh God, it's gone!"

Ishmael's response was the same again: "Where? Where?" When he got to Micah, he saw him standing feet apart, his hands clasped on top of his head, looking down *rue*fully at the ground. Soon Ishmael saw what was making his cousin look so mournful and dejected. The trap was entangled among some bushes. It had been dragged there from where it had been laid, but the 'visitor' had gone. Whatever animal it had caught had dragged it all the way, wrestled with it among the bushes, and escaped. It must have been a strong and sizeable animal.

Micah, moaned: "Look, see, just what I said. The stupid hedgehog has broken off one leg and hopped away."

Ishmael moved closer and saw all that the hedgehog had decided to leave them a paw and a bit of leg, which the trap was still clasping as faithfully and as fervently the whole hedgehog. "What a day! First one trap is exposed, and then this one is robbed. I wish we had come earlier, Mike." Characteristically, Ishmael recovered his *composure* more quickly. "Can't we trace it, Mike?" he asked.

"After struggling with this trap and dragging it all this way, the hedgehog must be very tired and may not be able to get far. It may still be quite near. Let's look for it. Any blood-stains?"

"Blood stains, my foot! You don't know hedgehogs, Ishie? I remember your father saying that with one good leg and three stumps, a hedgehog can get to Umuahia from here. You may try searching for it if you like, but remember that we have other traps to inspect, including the sling-traps and the weighted ones."

Undeterred, Ishmael walked back to where the trap had been laid to begin his tracking. The few blood-stains he could find were along the first few feet from the original position of the trap. He remembered that his father had taught them that these animals licked their wounds dry as they struggled for freedom, so he did not think that the blood-stains would help his search very much. He begged Micah to help. Micah agreed reluctantly, knowing that if he refused, they were bound to quarrel. Ishmael was very inconsiderate when anything had to do with fishing or trapping. He *brooked* no second opinion.

They set off, a matchet in one hand, a stick in the other. immediately to their right, beyond the entangled trap lay a valley, which ran for a long distance up and down the bush. They agreed that it was the most likely place for the hedgehog to have hobbled into in its bid for freedom. The first major decision about which they must not make a mistake, was the direction to take once they got inside that valley. The hedgehog could only have gone one way, up or down along the valley. Which way could it be? They went down on their knees and peered carefully around the bushes where the trap was entangled. They traced some fresh marks on the ground suggestive of dragging movements and also picked up a few spines and fur, thus convincing themselves with evident satisfaction that the animal had gone into that valley. But it was still going to be a tossup which direction they should follow. The side of the valley revealed nothing helpful. Whether the hedgehog had hopped into the valley or rolled over and over down the slope, they could find no *clue*. At the bottom of the valley, with the eye of faith rather than with any real evidence, they decided that the direction of the animal's getaway was northwards towards the deeper, more wooded end of the valley.

Making their way fairly fast, glancing up and down the sides of the valley, and scattering with their sticks or matchets or feet any suspicious heap of leaves, grass or twigs, they were soon getting into the deeper, damper, darker end of the valley. It was beginning to look like *a wild-goose chase* even to Ishmael. The light was not very good. The ground was wet with dew. The leaves underfoot were slippery. The place stank. They slowed down. A mixture of tiredness, disappointment and the stench of the dark valley was weighing them down. To make matters worse they found that their way was barred by a thick line of black and red soldier ants stretching right across the valley and up both sides. That was the limit. They turned wearily to trudge back home.

But suddenly, Ishmael remembered something. Soldier ants never match for nothing. They must be attacking something. What could it be? The hedgehog? He turned to

Micah: "Mike, remember what father said about soldier ants?"

"No, I don't. What did he say?" Micah grumbled.

"He said they never marched for fun."

"So?" Micah queried.

"Perhaps it's our hedgehog they are after."

"All right, you go ahead and get it from them." Micah taunted, losing his patience with Ishmael and his mad ideas.

"Well, I don't know. Perhaps we can't get it back. But we may see; we may know what has happened to it," Ishmael said without *conviction.*

"Go on then, Ishie, go on. I'm fed. I'm fed up. I'm tired. My eyes are rolling with hunger. My stomach is turning with this stench. I'm going home, going home, I repeat. I don't want

to eat your hedgehog, half-eaten by soldier ants.
Go, get it, have it all yourself. I'm going
home."

"Well, I'll go by myself. Perhaps I may find
it, I'll just follow the line of the soldier ants,"

Ishmael decided.

Micah grunted and continued on his way
homewards. Ishmael ignored his cousin. His
mind was on the soldier ants, which he hoped
would *pilot* him to his hedgehog. But Micah's
mind was not at ease. After walking a hundred
yards down the valley, he decided to go back to
his foolhardy young cousin. It would be awful if
he should come to any harm when it was known
that both of them had set out together. By the
time he arrived back at the line of the soldier
ants, Ishmael was already out of the valley
following them. Micah called out: "Ishie, wait
for me. I'm coming!" and he climbed out of the

valley in the same direction as the ants. He *broke into a trot* to catch up with Ishmael.

When he got to him he gave Ishmael a knock on the head and said: "You silly ass", feeling a bit better after that. Ishmael turned and gave him as dirty a look as he could muster, which was all he could do against Micah. He would not dare to challenge him to a fight, even at home where there might be people to part them when things proved difficult.

Together again, they continued their search, each of them *glum* for a different reason. Their quarrel was not deep and did not last long. They soon forget both their anger and their hunger. The soldier ant line meandered its way through the bush, here weaving away to skirt a tree, there dipping into a little hollow and up again. From time to time the two boys saw a mass of ants rolled up into a ball while the main line continued unbroken. They knew that those balls of ants were devouring some prey, but nothing they had seen so far could have been their hedgehog. Not even a baby hedgehog could have been so small. Besides, even small hedgehogs were such good fighters that their scampering and scratching was bound to disorganise the soldier ant line much more extensively. They ignored these interruptions and walked on, chatting amicably again.

The sun had come up a bit and it was beginning to get warm. Their conversation was all about trapping and fishing, *the ways and wiles of* the small animals they trapped, the character and cleverness of certain species of fish, their own trials and *tribulations* as young hunter's and, of course the occasional triumphs and excitements. They reminded themselves of good times in the past, Ishmeal's great catches of fish, their wonderful trapping successes which surprised even adults, and

Micah's catapulting feats. Micah was a good marksman. His most memorable success had been a hawk in flight, the really outstanding part of that occasion being that when the hawk landed it was still clutching the chick it had carried off. That chick survived and was rightly presented to Micah. It grew into a lovely hen and hatched many broods of chicks. Its offspring were widely sought after by people all over the village as the story had gotten around that these offsprings were safe from hawks. They made it sound as though the miraculous escape from the hawk had conferred an *immunity* on all its descendants. That *episode* had immortalized Micah's name, since all chicks traceable to that original one were thereafter referred to as: 'Micah's chicks'. The feat had never been repeated; adults who shot down hawks with their guns in similar circumstances always blasted the chicks to pieces at the same time.

The boys were still chatting away in this elated mood when they met their next obstacle. The soldier ant line widened and thickened, suggesting that there was an obstruction or a prey in front. They watched the line go a short distance up the trunk of a towering giant iroko tree and into a gaping cavity where part of the trunk had rotted and caved in. The sides of the caved-in portion had been axed for wood, but the main bulk of the trunk, many feet in diameter, remained untouched.

They had had enough now. All Micah's sourness welled up again. All the anger and the hunger returned, the heat making them worse. He turned and *glowered* at his cousin for a minute or so while searching for the most damaging remark to make. At last he found it:

"One day, Ishie, thus soldier ants will eat you up."

Having said that, he flung the stick he had been using for the search into the bush, clamped his matchet under his arm, and headed homewards again this time for good. After all, the other taps still had to be examined.

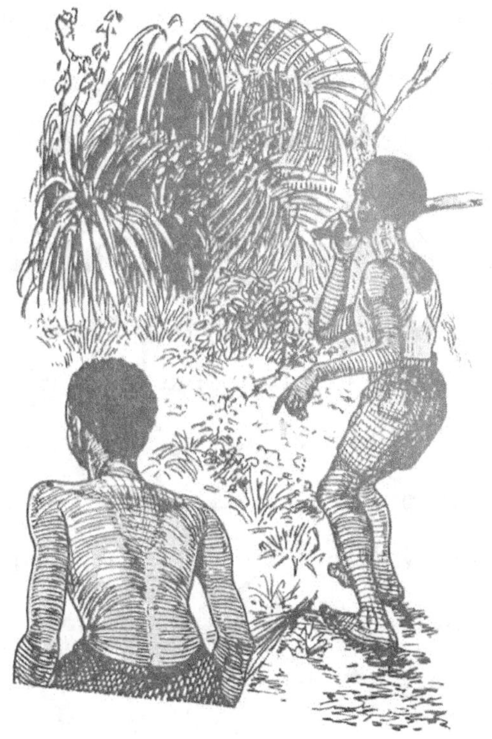

"One day, *Ishie, those* soldier *ants* will eat *you up.*"

As Ishmael stood their gazing into the iroko
tree, Micah threw him one final parting shot *to
rub in* his earlier remark: "Which do you want
to do now, Ishie, fell the iroko tree or jump
inside?"

Ishmael did not really notice either the
threat or the taunt. He was not even thinking of
his hedgehog anymore. He stood wondering
about the life and labours of the soldier ants,
their daring and their *devotion,* their *predatory*
sense and singleness of purpose. If it was a live
prey they had in that crevice, say a squirrel or a
rabbit, they had probably pursued it a long way.
If it was a dead one, did they smell it from the
other side of the valley? He shook his head
slowly in wonder at the soldier ants' amazing
organization and turned to go. He resolved to go
home.

He did not know how far Micah had gone,
but thought that if he ran, he could catch up

with him. He began running. Soon he saw Micah but he was still a long way off. As he got nearer he saw Micah in the characteristic attitude of someone trying to catch something unawares. He was stopped, treading *stealthily* and gingerly onwards something, his right arm raised and matchet poised not for cutting but for throwing.

As the noise of Ishmael's running disturbed the silence, Micah swung his left arm *viciously* back to give Ishmael silent command to be quiet. Ishmael obeyed, his heart thumping with new excitement. He did not know what his cousin was after, and would give anything to find out immediately. He tip-toed quietly but briskly towards his cousin and also raised his own matchet for a throw, should Micah miss his target, whatever it was. Even as Ishmael was still running through the various possibilities in his mind, Micah's matchet flashed towards its target, and Ishmael saw a large grey-and black-spattered partridge fly clumsily into the air towards the tall succulent grass grove to their right. Instinctively Ishmael let fly his own matchet at the airborne bird. 'Whoop' the matchet went through the air, bounced off the branch of a nearby tree and boomeranged towards Micah before either of them realized what was happening. Luckily the matchet had been deflected by the impact against the branch, and somersaulted on its way towards Micah. The handle hit him on the side of his right leg. He let out a wild laugh.

Ishmael thought it was a cry of pain, and ran trembling to his cousin, apologizing *profusely*. Micah *nudged* him aside and continued his inexplicable laughter. Ishmael stood dumbfounded. They had both missed the partridge, which could have been their only consolation for such a rotten morning. Micah had just narrowly missed being beheaded or at least being badly wounded. What had he got to laugh about? Ishmael shrugged and stood aside. He was far from amused.

When Micah recovered from his fit of laughter, he pointed to the bushy undergrowth in front of him and told Ishmael: "Collect the eggs." Ishmael came forward and looked. They were there, five brownish undersized eggs in a nest on the ground underneath an overhanging shrub. The partridge had been sitting on them. This seemed very poor recompense for missing the partridge. But what could they do?

While Ishmael was picking up the eggs, Micah suggested: "Let's go and collect your traps and then go home, Ishie."

"Not today, thank you. I want to go home. I'm famished. I'm tired. I'm fed up," Ishmael answered, and, almost as an afterthought, but quick as a flash, he added: "I don't want to be eaten up by the soldier ants."

Ishmael was inwardly happy. He had his own back on his cousin. It was all-square now, but he dared not show his feeling of pleasure.

8

Saturday Punishment

Ishmael and Micah got home to find that they were knee-deep in trouble. To be accurate, it was Ishmael who was in trouble. It was past eleven O'clock. Ishmael had therefore missed the Saturday work in the school premises, and it had been his group's turn that day. The work involved was only the arrangement of benches inside the Church for Sunday services and the *token* sweeping down the *aisle* and round the Church, but the boy in charge should have been there to take the names of any absentees.

He was also in trouble with his mother, who had waited in vain for Ishmael to return and accompany her and her other children to the farm. It was one of the days she was free from her own private farm-work, since her husband did not require their services on his own farm that day, and it was also not a market day. It had therefore been a disappointment to her to be short of one person in her limited labour force. She had, as was customary, concluded a mutual assistance agreement with the three other women whereby they helped one another their private farms *in rotation*. These women had all arrived with their children that morning, and Ishmael's absence was a letdown in the eyes of these people who had come to help her. In her anger, she had set Ishmael an alternative task which could take him the whole day. She left word with one of her fellow-wives that if Ishmael did not complete the task of cracking the two baskets of palm-nut he must be forbidden to join the order children on their popular Saturday afternoon angling. She also left word that Ishmael should find the ample breakfast she left for him in the *alcove* in the kitchen wall.

Ishmael's spirits sank. He hated the palm-nut cracking business. He felt the girls were always better at the boring task of pricking and cracking nuts on a stone slab one by one, *crouching* in the uncomfortable half-sitting, half-kneeling position. He could kick himself for his rotten luck that morning. Everything had decided to go *awry: the* blasted trap, the hateful hedgehog, the stinging valley, the wicked soldier ants, the confounded iroko tree, the clumsy partridge. He bore a *grudge* against all of them. How he wished that none of them existed! How he *yearned* for work in the Church premises or on the farm, in preference to this nut-cracking! He could have fallen down and cried; only it would not have helped.

Micah could not leave him to suffer alone after they had been on their wild-goose chase together. He offered to help out. Ishmael leapt for joy and thanked his cousin from the bottom of his heart. They then settled on the first items on the programme, breakfast. Ishmael brought out his breakfast from the alcove and they ate it quickly. After that, they went over to Micah's mother's kitchen by scaling the wall separating the family compounds, and did similar justice to the food they found there. Actually, scaling would be an exaggeration of the effort needed to get over the wall, for it had been so worn down by generations of *clambering* children that almost anyone could now stride over it at its lowest part.

Breakfast accomplished, Ishmael began mustering still further help for what was to him a Herculean task. He rounded up all the little cousins in both families, those who were not committed to anything in particular. He promised them fish and meat from his profitable pastime if they would help him crack the baskets of nuts. They all knew he *could make good* his *promises*, and no one hesitated. They followed him to his mother's backyard where there were several stone slabs and nut-crackers for the work, and set about the nuts. One sweet-voiced little girl led the orders in chorus while they cracked the nuts in *rhythm*. (Music while you work!) Ishmael was now freed. He watched the heaps of nuts *dwindle,* the heaps of shells grow and the baskets fill up gradually with the kernels. His heart glowed with the prospect of surprising his mother on her return by presenting her not with two baskets as she had ordered, but with three or even four if these children kept up their pace. His mother had plenty of food stored for entertaining her helpers at the end of the day's work. Ishmael therefore had no difficulty in getting enough food from the store and the kitchen, and also climbed into the barn for some

yams and coco-yams with which to feast his
team of cheerful helpers.

9

The Headmaster Speaks

Mr Obiako the church teacher, a bird-like, balding, middle-aged man, took the morning services as he usually did except when Mr Imo the Catechist was available. The Catechist covered four churches in his *circuit*, and so conducted the services in Amanzu only once a month, even though he lived there. During the services, Mr Obiako *stole the thunder of* Committee men, Jonas and Timothy when he read out, among other notices for the week, that the Headmaster wanted to meet the Committee of Church elders in his house after this morning service.

A mood of anxiety came over the *congregation,* certainly over those who had heard the rumours. The *ebullient* Jonas, who was not sitting near his friend Timothy, did his best to catch his friend's eye to give him that knowing nod which meant: "I told you so. People searched the sermon for any other hints from the preacher on the topic of the day. They were disappointed. The sermon was the same *stereotyped* exhortation of the congregation to lay up their treasure in heaven "where neither moth nor rust doth corrupt", instead of here on earth where they do; the same *admonition* to turn from their evil ways and live "like the apostles and the pastors", so that they would be "saved by the Lamb of God who taketh away the sins of the world".

The long session of lively exchange of greetings after the service gave Mrs Offor, the Headmaster's wife, sufficient time to arrange the benches brought from the Church to her house. She made the children put them in rows in her rear verandah. She was not going to be at the meeting, but she went to this trouble to ensure that there was enough seating accommodation to avoid the necessity of some of the Committee men dragging her precious cane chairs from the sitting room. The Committee men arrived expecting the news at once. Mr Offor gave them no news. He served them kola-nut and palm-wine traditional and down-to-earth. He exchanged greetings with some of them whom he had not seen immediately after the service. He chattered with them heartily about work, farming, the market and life in general. He had been Headmaster at Amanzu for over seven years and had also taught there in the early days of the school when it was only a group school and he was a pupil teacher. He knew these people *intimately,* knew they were fond of him and he knew he had been happy there. It was all he could do to keep up the appearance of *normality.*

Some of the Committee men were beginning to wonder whether their fears were unfounded after all. But this meeting was impromptu, so there must be something in it. Then, out it came. Mr Offor asked Matthew, the lay head of the Committee, if he remembered Mr Obioma, the Headmaster of Afara Central School. "Very well, H.M." Matthew answered, and continued: "We have met him at many joint Committee meetings, the last time being at ... em... Bende, wasn't it?"

Mr Offor had no doubt that Matthew would remember Mr Obioma. As leader of the lay members of the Committee, Matthew had often accompanied Mr Offor or Mr Obiako or both to joint meetings between the various churches in the district. "We know him too," chipped in the *rumbustious* Jonas. "Is he the one coming here?"

"Coming where, Jonas?" Mr offor asked, knowing in his heart that *the cat was already out of the bag*. Nevertheless, he had to give them his own version, the correct version. Jonas was one of those odd men, half clown, half hard-headed realist, who speaks first and thinks later. He went on, in spite of attempts by other Committee men to hush him: "H.M., we are not children to be given meat to eat before being told that our mother is dead. Even babes in arms have heard that you are leaving us. Tell it to us from your own mouth and let us go.",

"Enough, Jonas! Enough! Are you mad?" Matthew interrupted. "The H.M. is one of us and cannot deceive us." Then, turning to Mr Offor, Matthew added, "H.M.", as if introducing him to make a speech.

It worked. Not for the first time, the half clown, half-realist had brought things to a head. Mr Offor told them how Mr Simeon Obioma had, like St Paul on the way to Damascus, heard the voice of God calling him to serve. Mr Obioma was therefore going to train for the Ministry. He would undergo training in Calabar, in Lagos and then in Fourah Bay College, a great institution in a country called Sierra Leone. He would return as the Reverend Simeon Obioma to serve the Church. That would be an honour shared *by* the entire district. His new title would fit him too, considering the meaning of his name. (Obioma means 'good heat'.)

Mr Offor was aiming at softening the blow, and he hoped that this approach was achieving that end. He continued by telling them how, at a meeting of the Mission Education Committee held in Port Harcourt under the chairmanship of

the Manager, the Reverend William Jones, it
was decided that, as the Central School, Afara,
of which Mr Obioma was the Head, was the
most senior Central School, his successor must
be the most senior of the Headmasters in the
district. Mr Offor went on to say that in fact
Afara was more than a Central School. It was
partly a College, since a lower Elementary
Teacher Training course had been started there
two years ago. And so the Education
Committee's choice for this post happened to be
himself. He assured them that he was not going
away immediately. There was not going to be
the *indignity* of *hustling* him away in mid-term
from the school he had helped to build up. Mr
Obioma would be leaving for Calabar soon, as
his course was due to start in a fortnight's time.
Mr Obioma's Assistant would look after Afara
until he, Mr Offor, took over during the Easter
holidays. There was therefore plenty of time for
good-byes, he assured them.

As for his successor in Amanzu, the Education Committee had not chosen one, but he was sure they would soon choose and send the person best fitted to head the school. He was sorry about the way the rumours had gone about. It was all the fault of that public nuisance called the public letter-writer, Stanislaus Igiri. As they knew, a rumour about anyone usually missed the person it concerned, and he was often the last to hear about it. As it happened, this Stanislaus fellow had come and asked him point blank about 'the rumours' on Friday. He, Mr Offor, immediately dispatched one of the younger teachers to Umuahia to see Mr Dewar. The Supervisor of Schools had only received the papers from Port Harcourt that morning and had been *astonished* to hear that their contents were already known to Amanzu.

Mr Offor said he believed that the ex-convict Stanislaus must have agents in all the offices in the land, and probably bought stories from them. He warned his audience against that man who peddled rumours and *gossip*.

Finally he told them that he had been to see *Mr* Dewar on Saturday morning. He had told him that he was prepared to serve God anywhere and in any capacity.

"It may be," he joked, "that I may yet have the same call as my friend Mr Obioma has had. But whatever I may be, I shall always remember you, my friends," he concluded.

He had reduced them to the state of having no questions to ask. He had answered all possible ones. His audience remained silent, grave and rather blank. Matthew then spoke *in a tone of adjournment:* "H.M., thank you very much. We shall meet again on our own, and give you our reply."

Mr Offor thanked them again and they dispersed, leaving him wondering whether they were going to embark on that embarrassing gesture of writing a petition of protest to the Manager in Port Harcourt.

10

For He's a Jolly Good Fellow

The suspense of waiting for the announcement of who the new Headmaster was to be and where he was to come from was even more *distressing* to the school and the people of Amanzu than the fact of Mr Offor's leaving, now that it had been confirmed. Everyone seemed unhappy and uncertain about the future: the people, the teachers, especially Miss Chima who had been living with Mr and Mrs Offor, and older pupils, who understood what it meant to lose a Headmaster. Everyone forgot, in the general *surge* of goodwill, that Mr Offor was a hard taskmaster, keener on farming than on teaching, that had *archaic* methods of doing things, that he believed in the cane as much as any untrained teacher and encouraged his teachers to be unsparing in its use, and that both his pupils and his junior teachers had abominably poor results in external examinations. They chose to remember only that he had been in Amanzu a long time, that under him the school had been raised from a Group School with Standard Four as the top class to a Central School with Standard Six, and that he was very friendly with the townspeople.

Mr Offor was the one person who was not reacting to the events of the past weekend. On Monday morning he took the school Assembly in the Square with his accustomed military *precision*. He slapped anyone with uncut or unkempt hair, flinging them out of the lines for immediate unceremonious trimming by one of the burly Standard Six boys, who acted as 'executioner' on such occasions. He crunched up the ears of any pupil with dirt in or around the ears. He all but pulled out the teeth of anyone who had not used his chewing-stick properly, almost tore the finger nails off anyone with untrimmed ones, and stamped on the feet of those with untrimmed toe-nails. Finally, he flogged without mercy anyone in a dirty or torn school uniform. That was an assembly inspection, and it was routine. Having done this he marched the school, class by class, into the Assembly Hall where morning prayers were conducted by Mr Obiako, the Church teacher. After prayers and announcements the pupils retired *to* their various classrooms where people like Mr Okehi and other cane *happy* teachers took over, starting with the *roll call.*

In town the people prepared to give Mr Offor a send-off which would *go* on record as the best a Headmaster had ever received from a community he had served with distinction.

When Matthew made the *ominous* declaration that they would meet again on their own to make a decision, the last thing he had in mind was a protest petition to the Manager. He had in mind a *resounding* sendoff. Thus far, therefore, Mr Offor's suspicion was unfounded.

Matthew summoned a meeting in his house on Tuesday evening. He invited prominent people in the community. As Tuesday was a big market day, farm work would be practically *in abeyance*, and Matthew expected a good turn-out. He also reckoned that the people would attend readily because they could expect lavish entertainment whatever the deliberations.

Matthew's calculations were all correct. Everyone invited attended. As usual, most people arrived late, but they did come. There were also the inevitable gate-crashers. Matthew was a rich gunpowder and tobacco merchant, and his wife prepared and sold tobacco and snuff as well as small rolled tobacco leaves. Gate-crashers came under the pre-*text* of wanting to buy tobacco or snuff or to pay little debts they owed Matthew or his wife. After buying their cover-up articles or paying their petty debts, naturally they went in *to 'pay their respects* to the big man'. They were invariably offered a drink which they accepted *demurely,* all the time proclaiming their innocence.

Matthew was neither deceived nor did he care. He always had the measure of such men. When all the men he had invited arrived and he deemed it time to turn to the business for the evening, he summarily dismissed the gate-crashers.

As on Sunday morning in the Headmaster's house, the drinks had put everyone in a receptive mood. The decisions they arrived at were therefore friendly and far-reaching, even if the discussions were *loquacious* and long-winded.

Perhaps the most revolutionary of the items on the programme of activities drawn up for the Headmaster's send-off was the hiring of a lorry to take him and his family and belongings to his new school.

The meeting for the *HM send-off party* went well

One *snag* was that the lorry could not quite get to the new school. It could get to a point on the Bende road about three and half miles from the school, but that was the best they could do. Labourers could be hired to complete

the transportation of the luggage. The hiring of a lorry was an expensive undertaking. They felt sure their gesture would impress Mr Offor and everybody else. Mr Offor deserved the full V.I.P. treatment. Until then, the traditional transport arrangements for teachers or even Catechists going on transfer involved *mutual* agreement between the two schools or parishes exchanging personnel. Selected pupils or selected parishioners transported the luggage on their heads the whole distance or the two groups met halfway and exchanged their loads. If this *rendezvous* method was agreed upon, woe be tide the team which did not make an allowance for the incoming teacher or Catechist having more luggage than the outgoing one. They would be loaded like pack-horses.

Other less momentous decisions made at the meeting in Matthew's house centered around the gifts to be made to the Headmaster and his wife. These included goats, two or three big he-goats for slaughter and some g young female ones for rearing, and a number of poultry, also of both categories, for the table and for rearing. That was as far as domestic animals went. Yams headed the list of foodstuffs too numerous to recount. No the wander the pupils rarely looked forward to teachers' transfers. The presents, not the teachers' personal possessions, made up the bulk of the luggage.

Someone suggested arranging a wrestling match to entertain the Headmaster. It was roundly condemned by another person as 'primitive'. Matthew, in opposing the suggestion of a wrestling match, stressed that he did not consider it primitive, but that it invariably provoked much bad blood between the wrestlers and among their supporters, and was therefore not suitable for an occasion such as a pleasant send-off for their good friend. He did not forget *to pour scorn on* the person who described as primitive the wholesome and healthy sport of wrestling. He said that he pitied those people who were prepared to throw overboard everything that was theirs in favour of things foreign. In his opinion, twenty or thirty people chasing and kicking a football round the field looked more primitive and childish. "How does that show who is a man?" he asked.

In place of a wrestling match, it was agreed to ask the women to stage a folk dance. Dancing by the men was out of the question, since some of the traditional dances had been *proscribed* by the Church as idolatrous and were largely forgotten, while the surviving yam-festival dances would be out of place during the planting season.

On the home front, the Assistant Headmaster, Mr Mozie, was organizing the school for their own demonstration of loyalty and appreciation. At a meeting of the teachers that week, a programme was drawn up, less *heroic* than that drawn up by Matthew and his team, but colourful and comprehensive all the same. It included, among other items, a school concert, a special physical training demonstration, a football match between the School XI and Second XI, to be played, not on that dust-bowl which was the school Square, but on a proper football field in town. There was to be a group photograph of the whole school. For a present, the teachers were to order a special easy chair, made entirely of cane and raffia. It was to have a detachable foot-rest on which meals could be served. Someone had seen this unique chair in Ikot Ekpene, and the teachers would raise the money to buy it.

11

The Public Letter-Writer

No one had *reckoned* with the *enigmatic* Stanislaus Igiri, the public letter-writer, nor with the brash and talkative Committee man, Jonas.

Stanislaus was not at heart an evil man, but his restless mind and his *flights of fancy* always drove him to stir up one trouble after another. He had been a promising young court interpreter and was considered a very learned one because of his *polysyllabic* and high-sounding language which he lifted straight out of his three volume dictionary. No one could find the words he used in the simpler dictionaries available in the courtrooms. At first it was fun. Then, as he became sought after by plaintiff and defendant alike, he began manipulating his interpretations according to which party 'saw' him first. As the habit caught on, he went *into the final plunge of* taking bribes from both sides. He was caught, given a taste of the defendant's stand, jailed and dismissed from the service. After his stint in the District Headquarters prison in Bende, he came to Amanzu with his dictionaries, and set up as a public letter-writer.

He played havoc with people's letters and telegrams, but was never out of work. His charges were moderate; one penny for letters and two pence for telegrams. He made his money on petitions, and petitions were common in those days when the authorities were scarcely *accessible* by any other means. For petitions his charges varied with importance of the subject and the length of the petition; and to help himself *he spared* no *pains* to make sure that the petitions were *verbose*, however trivial the subject matter. Stanislaus was also something of a mobile bookshop. He *peddled* all sorts of obscure, abstruse and obscene books; books on dreams, palmistry, faith-healing, American Wild West stories, conjuring tricks, Indian Yoga, and also talismans. He travelled widely to sell these things and make contacts. No doubt in his travels he picked up news and passed it or. No wonder the Headmaster had referred to him as the public nuisance.

Stanislaus was nevertheless a very likable person. He was in his late twenties, light in build, *fair* in complexion, with fine facial features and hair combed forward. He was rather bow-legged and was always *meticulously* neat. He wore white shorts showing a touch of parade ground ironing; white short sleeved shirts with the sleeves given an extra turn-up, the corner of a white handkerchief peeping out of one of his short pockets, and an array of pens and pencils displayed on his shirt pocket. He resembled one of the so-called Calabar dandies, but he did not come from Calabar. With his breezy nature, his apparent interest in everything around, and his engaging talk, he had friends everywhere.

He had no difficulty in finding out whatMr Offor told the Committee men (his informer, Jonas), and he also found out about the plans in the village for Mr Offor's sendoff and even the programme of activities drawn up in the school. But he soon discovered that he could not make capital out of the Headmaster's impending transfer. He could not stir the townspeople into writing a petition against Offor's transfer. Mr Offor had explained it to them so well. Even the rumbustious Jonas agreed that it could not be done.

For once this merchant of ideas, Stanislaus, seemed to have run dry of them. He just could not think of anything. But help came to him from a quite unexpected quarter. He was at that time what he called 'flush', which meant having plenty of money in his lands. He was a bachelor, and therefore went the town to spend e money on the only thing he cared for, clothes. He went to his tailor and friend, the renowned 'London Boy' Philemon, to order a few more white shirts and shorts.

There, conversation drifted naturally to the Central School, since Philemon was also the school tailor. After Mr Offor's transfer came Philemon was far from happy about it, having held the job of school tailor by virtue of the Headmaster's *patronage*. "Are there people petitioning about it yet?" he asked.

"Not in your life!" Stanislaus exploded. "And there isn't *the ghost* of a *chance* that they will budge. They seem content to let him go with all the goats and fowls and yams they have got in this place." Then he proceeded to tell Philemon, word for word, all he had heard about the Headmaster's explanation of the situation and about the plans for the send -off.

Philemon shook his head slowly, pitifully.

"No petition? " he asked.

"No, no petition".

"That's terrible. Have you heard who's coming?"

"Who? Who?" Stanislaus shouted agitatedly, nearly falling off the tailor's worktable on which he had been perching.

"I don't know. I was only asking if you had heard." Philemon answered calmly. "Oh!" Stanislaus groaned. "I thought you had heard.

I wonder who it will be. I know all the Headmasters around here. I know the one at...."

"Stanny," Philemon called, interrupting his friend's *soliloquy,* "Stanny, what if these people don't like the new Headmaster they are sent; can't they protest then and ....?" ad

"That's it, London Boy! That's it! I've got it! I've got it! I know what I'll do now,' Stanislaus shouted. His thought-block had been broken by his friend's incomplete suggestion. It all became clear in his mind. He would work up those people against the new Headmaster.

It ought to work, he told himself.

"It must work," he said out aloud. "What must work, Stanny?" Philemon asked.

Stanislaus did not hear his friend's question. He was already framing the petition in his mind.

Most of the petitions he wrote for people were practically ghost-written by him. All he required from them was a general idea of their grievance, and then their signatures or thumb-prints at the end.

When he got home that afternoon Stanislaus worked out the plan of his campaign. It was to be in two phases. First, he would work on the Committee through some of his friends, convincing them that a petition need not be a complaint or a protest and that they could write one which would be in effect a testimonial of good conduct for the outgoing Headmaster. Such a petition would also portray them in a very good light as kind, appreciative and noble people. If they fell for this, he would stay poised to bring in the second praise as was due. It wouldn't matter if they considered him unsuitable. If they did this, they could not be accused of being difficult people, since it would be evident that they gave praise where praise was due. Stanislaus felt satisfied with himself.

Mrs Offor soon found that winding up her affairs in Amanzu was not going to be easy. Her husband's task was comparatively simple. He had two large arms and was sure he could arrange for someone to look after them until the harvest season later in the year. He did not worry unduly about the school farm which was in effect, if not in name, also his own. It was not really a rich farm in spite of the manure lavished on it.

By contrast, Mrs Offor had grown into a serious business woman in town. After giving up petty trading in the market (considered beneath the dignity of a Headmaster's wife), she had taken out sub-agencies with two of the commercial houses in town for retail trading in soap and salt. From the West African Trading Company (W.A.T.C), she got the soap business;

Mr G. Brown-Wilcox, her townsman who was a junior Assistant Manager in the firm, standing security for her. By virtue of her standing with W.A.T.C., she secured the second business, in salt, from the Nigerian Merchant Ventures (N.M.V.).

It was no surprise that she had such business *acumen*. She came from Opobo, a good breeding ground for business-women. She had married Mr Offor when he was teaching in the Group School at Egwanga, Opobo. She had two young women living with her who actually handled the soap and the salt, albeit briefly. Mrs Offor herself merely signed for them, her girls were there to sell the soap or salt in bulk to local traders waiting on the steps of the shops.

Her husband's counsel on the matter of folding up or re-negotiating her trading concerns was not very helpful. He declared that he was first and foremost a teacher, that farming was his hobby, but that he lacked the instinct for trading. His suggestions were impracticable as they were *naive*. These included getting one of their friends to look after the business, and asking the firms concerned to send the necessary documents to his new station for his wife's signature. The truth was that his mind was not on the problem. He lived in fear of the Mission authorities finding out about his wife's business interests, and was thankful that, so far, Amanzu people had been so well disposed to him that they had not petitioned the Reverend *Mr* Jones about the way his wife was laying up her treasure here on earth'.

Mrs Offor knew about her husband's fears. She thought they were silly but dared not say so. *She* toyed with the idea of staying on at Amanzu to look after her growing business. On second thoughts, however, she abandoned the idea. It would not work. It would blow the matter right open, and set tongues wagging. Above all, it would be *the height of folly* to let her husband live alone even among the relatively unsophisticated women of Afara. You could not trust these men farther than you could see them!

Mrs Offor's only other *confidant* was Miss Chima.

"Miss," she said in a low confident tone when she found her, "have you heard what Sammy's father suggested?" (Mrs Offor always referred to her husband in that way; Sammy, for Samuel, being their first son.)

"What Ma?" Miss Chima asked.

"He believes we can find someone in this town to sign my shop papers for me after we have gone. What do you think?"

Ma', the shops may not agree. Besides, who can you trust to do it for you?"

"You are right, Miss. People are so unreliable.

"Miss, have *you heard what Sammy's* father *suggested*?"

"She dared not tell Miss Chima that the only person she could have entrusted with that responsibility was Miss Chima herself. Mrs Offor knew if her husband was so scared of the official reaction to trading with these firms, poor Miss Chima had every right to be doubly frightened. She realised that even though Miss Chima had grown immeasurably mature and confident since her training, it would be unfair *to saddle her with* a risky responsibility well beyond her eighteen years.

The conversation, which had not been very animated, drifted to other subjects. But soon Miss Chima returned to the topic with the suggestion that Mrs Offor should explore the possibilities of arranging with the shop managers for her to sign her documents in the shops once a month when she could come up from her new station. She said it would involve slight delays of the consignment of goods in the shops, but if the Managers were co-operative, they might be persuaded to agree.

This was one possibility Mrs Offor had not considered. She had thought of asking to open a small branch for these goods in Afara, but realized there would be no motor road to bring them in.

She hugged Miss Chima warmly as she would have hugged a daughter had she had one (she had five sons), and thanked her for her suggestion which she would certainly follow up immediately.

Trust obstacles to come up at the worst times! Mrs Offor soon discovered that she could not follow up Miss Chima's bright suggestions very far. The friendly and experienced W.A.T.C. Manager had recently gone on leave. The new Manager was a younger, colder man who did everything correctly according to the book. He was prepared to overlook the slight irregularity of Mrs Offor not paying the required cash security for the soap transaction, but was definitely not going to allow any *concessions* which might clog up his shop with soap waiting the pleasure of Mrs Offor's clearance. The W.A.T.C. arrangement was her anchor and security for the salt trade with N.M.V. With this second firm, therefore, even with the original Manager available, the proposed monthly clearance could not be arranged. Mrs Offor was disappointed.

If only fate could have brought together Stanislaus, who was raring to go at his pet pastime-cum-occupation, petition writing, and Mrs Offor, who would have paid anything to stay on at Amanzu with her husband, it might have become possible to whip up a: 'Keep our Headmaster' movement in the town. But fate did not bring them together.

The first move in Stanislaus' grand design was an unqualified success. It pleased and surprised him. Matthew and his Committee men fell for it, hook, line and sinker. They thought it was a first class idea sending this 'testimonial' to the Reverend William Jones without Mr Offor's knowledge. The fact that the suggestion had been brought up by the *erratic* Jonas did not arouse anyone's suspicion. It was typical of Jonas *to* come up with the most *ingenious* idea or with the most naive, the chances being even.

If Jonas had pressed on by suggesting Stanislaus as the obvious letter writer to engage, he might have ruined the game. For once, however, he held his tongue. One of the other Committee men put it to the meeting that, though they had no choice as to who should write the petition for them, they must warn Stanislaus to keep his mouth shut after writing it. "In fact, he ought to be sworn to secrecy," he ended. "We don't swear anyone to secrecy. We are Christians," Matthew objected. "Asking him to keep his mouth shut is like asking him to stop breathing. He can't do either until he is dead. But we must ask him not to write those very long words people say he writes and boasts about. The Manager, Mr Jones, won't like to read that sort of thing....'

"He should like it," someone butted in, interrupting Matthew. "He is educated himself, isn't he, this Reverend Jones?"

"Well they say that really educated people prefer simple words," Matthew answered. "I don't agree," returned the other man, standing his ground. "Who formed the long words? Certainly not Stanislaus. They must have been formed in England. Why should the Manager be afraid of long English words."

"All right, Samson, that will do," Matthew decreed.

"That's not what we are here to settle. Let us get this man Stanislaus and tell him exactly

156

what to write. Then we shall ask him to make a draft of the petition and read it to us. If it is good, we shall ask him to go ahead and write the full thing. Is that not as it should be, my friends?" Matthew asked quasi-democratically.

"It is! It is!" the Committee men chorused.

The draft was ready, except for the names of the Committee men, but when Stanislaus officially received his commission to do the work, he went painstakingly through the movements of taking rather detailed notes at the briefing in Matthew's house. Then he let four days *go* before telling Matthew that the draft was ready. It made for interesting reading, or rather, interesting hearing. It went like this:

"From the Principality and People of Amanzu in Bende

District in Owerri Province,

Through their Honourable and highly Esteemed Committee of Church Elders assembled, To the Right Reverend William B. Jones, B. A. (Hons.).

B.D., Dip. Ed., Magnanimous Manager of Mission Schools,

Our dear and beloved Reverend,

Greetings....."

There followed long-winded passages of disjointed facts and *assertions*. The letter traced the history of Amanzu and of the Christian missionaries in the country. It praised Mr Jones, Mr Offor and the people of Amanzu in turn, reserving the cream of the praise for Mr Offor. There was nothing left unsaid about Mr Offor. Some of the remarks were overtly or covertly damaging to Mr Offor, but Stanislaus maintained his barrage of high-sounding words throughout. At last, he closed the letter as he opened it, bombastically:

"We have the honour and integrity to remain,

Your fastidious followers of the Faith:

Big Matthew Abosi: Committee Leader X His Mark

John Oji: Committee Member X His Mark

Marcus Obike: Committee Member X His Mark

Timothy Chukwu: Committee Member X His Mark"

and so it went until all the Committee men had been listed.

During his reading of the draft petition, there were murmurings about the length but little criticism of its contents. Stanislaus was happy. The translation he made, phrase by phrase, sounded satisfactory. At the end, the applause was quiet but unanimous. Once more he was urged to keep the matter secret under pain of withdrawal of patronage. He was paid in advance and asked to write the full petition and bring it up for signatures or thumb-prints.

The petition was to be lodged with Matthew for eventual forwarding to the Reverend Williams Jones after Mr Offor's departure.

12

The New Headmaster

The next development in the Central School story caught Stanislaus *napping*. That was a change. The ink was scarcely dry on his petition when the story blew right open again. On Tuesday morning, both Mr offor and Mr J. O. Mozie left the school to ride to Umuahia at the invitation of the Supervisor of Schools. This started off another *spate of rumours* of closure of the school, of reduction in status, or cancellation of the Headmaster's transfer, of more transfers to come, of a quarrel between the Headmaster and his Assistant. Everyone tried his hand at *prophesying*.

In an emergency meeting of the Church Committee the following day Mr Offor killed the new rumours. He was in his most engaging mood. He told the Committee men that his successor had been named and was someone they would like very much, someone they knew. "Thank God!" They sighed. But who? They wondered. They gasped when he announced the name Mr Mozie, his assistant.

Hard as he tried *to extol the virtues of* Mr Mozie, whom the Education Council meeting in Port Harcourt had chosen to succeed him, Mr Offor saw pain and disappointment written plainly on the faces of his audience. That Mr Mozie was very clever and had got the Senior Teacher's certificate in two subjects meant little to them. Mr Offor strove to explain why he believed that Mr Mozie could bring as much *credit* and honour to the school as he himself had done, but they were not impressed. Urging them to cooperate with and help the young Headmaster, and begging them not to hinder any changes he might seek to introduce, sounded like *rubbing salt* into *an open* wound. Mr Offor was worried. He had known that it would be difficult to bring these people to accept such a young man as Headmaster. Mr Dewar had foreseen it too, hence he had invited Mr Offor to Umuahia to delegate to him the diplomatic task of *selling the idea to* his Committee. He was not succeeding yet, but he was determined to thrash out the matter with them. He asked them for their opinion, to uphold for turning *to* Matthew first.

"Eh*!* H.M., an unmarried Headmaster?" Samson asked in *exasperation* before Matthew could say a word. "It's not only that, H.M.," Matthew came in eventually. "There are many points. That boy is too young. You say that he is very clever. We can take your word for it. He may also be good at teaching, but it is said that he is too soft with the pupils. We don't want our children to grow wild and *headstrong*. If he is afraid to flog the children, how can they learn? They say he reads too much. If so, he cannot be interested in us; he cannot mix with us, crack jokes with us or help us in many little ways as you do. He has now been in Amanzu for more than three years. How many of us here has he visited?"

"None! None!" they chorused, and then began to talk among themselves.

Matthew broke into their subdued muttering, while Mr Offor sat back looking as *genial* as he could: "You see, H.M., if he was a person we did not know, the chances would have been better. Why couldn't the Manager send us someone new, even if he wasn't so clever; someone we could receive and start with afresh, a man of the people, a humble man?

"Samson here thinks that this young man's lack of a wife is the most important point against him. That is nonsense. He can get married during the Easter holidays before he takes over. That's simple. There are many pretty girls here in Amanzu, and there must be many girls in Awka. That's where he comes from, isn't it?"!

"That's what they say," someone grumbled.

Samson let out one monumental *guffaw* and then asked: "What of the little lady teacher down in the school?"

Others glowered at him disapprovingly and Samson shut his eyes, unable to face them. Mr Offor let them bring up all their objections there and then. He reckoned it was the best possible way of avoiding further *agitation* at a later date. When they had exhausted their *repertoire* of objections and complaints, he took over. He assured them that he would raise the question of marriage with Mr Mozie, but that it was really not important, as he could vouch that Mr Mozie was a man of exemplary character. He further assured them that the new *Headmaster* would do his best to uphold the prestige of the school, and that they would find him much less 'aloof and snobbish than *they* were imagining. Finally, he promised them that, from his new school, he would continue to keep his interest in their welfare and his eye on their school.

Even the sound and dependable Matthew did not seem as though he had been won over by Mr Offor. However, he accepted, on behalf of the Committee, that they would give the man a try. Some of the other members still shook their heads sorrowfully at the end of the meeting.

The Committee men adjourned to Matthew's house to discuss whether or not the new element introduced called for further action. They agreed it would be *a stab in the back*, if, after accepting Mr Offor's assurances, they failed to keep their own part of the bargain.

Reconsideration of the petition already being written by Stanislaus proved rather thorny. It was agreed in the end that it was still relevant.

Meanwhile the school programme of activities for the Headmaster's send-off was being prepared. There were rehearsals almost every evening for the concert. The school had been divided into four groups for this purpose, the division being roughly into age groups. The infant classes were in groups, then Standards One and Two, Standards Three and Four, and Standards Five and *Six* in the other groups. The various groups were supervised by their respective monitors, the only intervention from the teachers being the advice given through the monitors that they should avoid the usual *pantomime* pattern of school concerts which *satirized* the staff, not sparing the Headmaster. Whether their advice would be heeded remained to be seen.

The arrangements for the Physical Training demonstration had stalled on the choice of items for the demonstration. General marching, press-ups, cart-wheeling, somersaults and leap-frog had all been agreed on. The dispute was over 'O'Grady says: This item was a test of alertness and presence of mind in which pupils were penalized if they obeyed any drill orders not preceded by 'O'Grady says', or failed to obey orders preceded by it. Normally, the penalty was swift and sure, a 'swish' over the shoulder with a cane.

Mr Ibe, the Standard Four teacher, suggested that for the special demonstration,

'O'Grady says' should be modified, making it an elimination drill, with pupils who faltered standing out rather than being caned. He argued that caning would not be in accordance with the spirit of the day. But blister-thirsty Mr Agomuo would have none of it. He contended that it would irk the Headmaster to watch his favourite drill item being ruined even before he had turned his back.

"Further," he argued, "if you dropped pupils out instead of caning them, you would end up not having enough pupils to carry on the drill."

There was sense in both arguments, and when they failed to resolve the dispute, the matter was referred to Mr Mozie.

13

A Match to Remember

There was great excitement about the football match. Mr Agomuo had little difficulty in securing the field on which his club, the Wanderers, played regularly. The match was fixed for the following Friday. It was meant to be a friendly match, but as everyone knew, if a match was friendly, it could not be football, and *vice versa*. Steps were therefore taken beforehand to minimize the chances of the proposed match developing into *a double pitched battle* on the field, and among the spectators. A second reason for extra *precautions* was that the First XI, though no champions, were vastly superior to the Second

XI and it was not proposed to stage the match as a 'massacre of the innocents'. That would be *courting tragedy*, as nothing would be more likely to fray tempers on and off the field than a one-sided game. The inclusion of some members of the staff in each team was considered and then dropped. Mr Agomuo argued that it would not substantially reduce the risk of a *brawl*. It might even increase that risk.

In the end Mr Agomuo was surprised by the majority decision of the members of the staff that he should play center half for the Second XI to *reinforce* the team and exercise a *stabilizing* effect on the match. Any opportunity to play football *thrilled* him, but he thought it was *absurd* that he should play with children. He was much too good and much too big for them, but he saw the point his colleagues were making and agreed.

Mr Mozie liked the idea of Mr Agomuo bolstering the Second XI. He decided to add further colour to the match by asking Mr Obiako, the church teacher, to referee the match. Mr Obiako was the oldest teacher in the school, older even than the Headmaster. He was a *dapper* little scholarly man, and no great sportsman. He had never refereed any contest more complicated than a wrestling match in the school sand-pit. But Mr Mozie knew that Mr Obiako's *sense* of *fair play* was *puritanical*, and, once he was made to understand something about refereeing a football match, he could be trusted to see that the players did not pluck each other's eyes out.

Friday was a market-day in town. The *story* that Mr Agomuo would be playing had got around, and, as he had quite a number of fans among the young traders, it could be said that the early breaking up of part of the market that day was due to him. The women and the older men, however, continued in the market. What business had they had with school children kicking themselves and a chunk of leather round and round the field?

Admission to the field was free. School children from the nearby St Luke's Roman Catholic School attended *in force* and so did other children from the town. The turn-out from the Central School was practically a hundred per cent. The match had all the semblance of an inter-school challenge match. All the frills were there, down to smear schoolgirls peeling oranges and arranging them on cane-handled trays for serving the referee, the linesmen and the players at half time. At ten to five promptly, Mr Obiako, in white shirt, white trousers (rare for him on a weekday) and white canvas shoes, blew his whistle, assembled both teams, and marched them and the linesmen to salute the

Headmaster who was seated under a canopy erected for the occasion. He then marched them back to the middle of the field. Next, Mr Mozie handed the Headmaster a shiny new ball for the kick-off. Mr Offor tucked the competently under his left arm, and strode out of his 'Royal box' on the edge of the field. His white shorts, starched and ironed stiff as always, were *immaculate* in the bright sunshine. As spectators and players began to clap, he threw the ball into the air and kicked it sure-footed and with all his strength high over the middle of the field, amidst thunderous applause.

The glory of that mighty kick was short-lived. Mr Offor was seen to bend down immediately and grip his ankle. He had overdone it. The new bail was too hard to have been treated with the same respect which Mr Offor had shown it. He had *sprained* his ankle. But he was too tough a man to demonstrate pain in public. He straightened up again almost as soon as he touched his ankle, and strode back as honourably as he could. Mr Mozie was there to attend to him. He loosened the Headmaster's shoe and put up the injured foot on a low stool. Mr Offor refused to consider going back home to have the ankle properly strapped. Mr Mozie therefore dashed back to the school to get bandages.

Mr Offfor threw Mr Offfor threw the ball into the air *and kicked* it

Before he returned, Stanislaus helped to support the Headmaster's ankle with three knotted handkerchiefs.

Meanwhile the great match went on. The toss was taken. The First XI won and naturally chose to play with the sun on their backs. The field sloped a little from left to right, so they had the additional advantage of playing downhill in the first half. A further advantage in winning the toss was that they kept their white sleeveless vests on while the other team shed theirs to distinguish the two teams. The solitary and momentary advantage in losing the toss was kicking off in the first half. In the second half, all the roles were reversed, down to the wearing of vests by the team *deprived* of theirs in the first half.

Within three minutes, Mr.Agomuo hit the on crossbar of the First XI goal from the center of the field. The cross-bar, neither strong nor k level, but sagging considerably in the middle, rocked tremulously and let the ball bounce behind the goal. With that near miss it looked as if Mr Agomuo's presence was going to prove a great handicap to the First the XI.

Mr Agomuo had not liked the stripping act, and he tied a large white handkerchief around his neck. He tore up and down the field as if he were playing an inter-provincial match with a trophy at stake. His team loved his act. They seemed content to leave the game to him. He was, after all, their only hope.

The First XI soon saw how totally dependent on him his team-mates were and decided on a very good move. As Mr Agomuo came down on one of his solo rampages on their side, their center half passed back to the goalkeeper who promptly kicked the ball high into the mid-field. The First XI center forward, Christian, trapped the ball and raced towards goal. Mr Agomuo wheeled around and gave chase. Meanwhile the rest of the defence was drawing back instead of *tackling* Christian. The left back, Gregory, kept shouting: "Sir, come back! Sir, come back!" while retreating blindly. His goal-keeper yelled: "Give way! Give way!" but, unheeding, Gregory continued his retreat until Bang! He crashed into the goalkeeper. Christian had no difficulty in tapping the ball over the sprawled pair and into the goal. The crowd roared.

That did it. Mr Agomuo sobered up and returned *to knit* his team together. With such a shaky defence, he could ill afford to forage for goals. If his timid forwards could not score, that was just too bad.

That goal spurred the First XI on. They tried hard to score again, but could do nothing to pass Mr Agomuo in mid-field. He more than made up for the deficiency of the rest of his defence, but his forwards were without hope, and never looked like scoring.

Soon Christian and his team switched to wing play to avoid Mr Agomuo. They concentrated their passes to the wings, swinging the ball low from one side to the other. They reckoned that, if Mr Agomuo could be drawn to chase the ball to one wing, the center would once more be open. But Mr Agomuo would not be drawn. He moved no further on either side than was *compatible* with early recovery should the ball be switched to the other side. He succeeded in keeping the raiders at bay. The strain was nevertheless telling on his other defenders, and in the twenty-second minute, the *diffident* left back, Gregory, came to the aid of the First XI again. As Christian, wandering to the right wing, swung the ball hip-level towards the middle, Gregory handled it in the penalty area.

"Penalty! Penalty!" the crowd decided, and penalty it was. After the uproar *of* the unanimous decision, followed the breath-holding silence for the 'execution'. The referee's shortish twelve steps to the 'spot' helped Christian, or maybe it would have made no difference. Christian made no mistake. He tapped the fast moving new ball low to the left corner of the goal. The goalkeeper dived correctly, but could not get there in time. The crowd roared again. They loved goals.

Two goals down and six minutes to go to half-time. Mr Agomuo was downcast. His lame forwards kicked off again. He thought of making one desperate fling to score before the interval, but each time he moved up leaving the defenders, they began chanting: "*Sir*, come back!' He turned angrily and snapped: "Shut up, you fools!' Mr Obiako turned and firmly put his forefinger to his lips for a silent but stern: "Shut up too!' to the furious Mr Agomuo. He apologized with a curt salute.

While this was happening, Christian was leading his boys into the Second XI goal area again. Mr Agomuo was frantic. He bounced back, and in the nick of time, intercepted both ball and boy dangerously near his goal for a corner. Corner or another penalty? The referee decided on a corner, but tugged demonstratively at his own ear to indicate to Mr Agomuo that he was not heeding his warning. The right winger took the corner, lifting the ball foolishly into the air. There was only one person in it when it came to a ball in the air Mr Agomuo. He headed the ball clear, followed it up, and lifted it again first bounce towards the opposite goal. There was no one on his side to follow the ball further, but Mr Agomuo felt relieved to have stopped another goal.

Mr Obiako's handling of the game had been *austere* without slowing it down. Incidents on the field were few and far between, and by half-time every player was still unharmed.

The second half started with the same blistering pace, as had the first. Mr Agomuo's team, or, more correctly, Mr Agomuo himself, was still in a fighting mood. All the advantages were now on his side: the sun, slope, and the vests. He had given his team a pep talk during the interval, and decided to reorganize them for the second half. The nervous blundering left back, Gregory was the main reason for the positional changes. He was *moved to* inside left while the inside forward dropped to left half and the more dependable wing half replaced Gregory at left back. Whatever else Gregory did upfield, he would not earn them another penalty or bump into the goal-keeper.

The move worked, and with Mr Agomuo playing his heart out, the First XI was thrown back on the defensive. Still, no goals came for the Second XI. None came because everyone in the team was expecting Mr Agomuo to score for them, and played as though there was an understanding that, if he did not score, no one else should. It must have exasperated poor Mr Agomuo to see all the scoring chances wasted by his incompetent forwards!

Ten minutes passed before the First XI recovered their rhythm of play. They switched once more to the tactics, which put them on top in the first half, and attacked, from the wings. This forced Mr Agomuo to beat a hasty retreat and soon his team lost their temporary domination. The score remained 2-0.

For the next five minutes or so the players swirled round in clusters that formed, broke up, and re-formed as they scrambled for the ball from one wing to the other in the Second XI half of the field. The pressure was on again and it looked as if the third goal would not be long in coming.

Suddenly Mr Agomuo bullied his way out of the *melee* in front of his goal-mouth, taking the ball with him and dashed down the field towards the other goal. Everyone ran after him, team-mates and opponents alike. He sped past the remaining First XI defender who had not moved up into the attack and with only the advancing goal-keeper to beat, let out a full-blooded right-footed shot which looked like a goal the moment it left his foot. The poor goal-keeper put up a knee and both arms more in defence than in an effort to save the shot, closing his eyes as he did so. The ball floored him, but whizzed off mercifully for a corner.

Mr Agomuo's jubilant leap after he hit the ball was frozen in mid-air when he saw the *calamity*. When he landed, more heavy footed than on take-off, he beat his chest, in despair.

He looked towards the goal-keeper, not wishing him well. The boy had scampered off and broken into a victory dance. He was now back at his goal, Ready to face a thousand corner kicks from fellow mortals rather than one of those thunderbolts from Mr Agomuo.

Mr Agomuo was still *seething with rage,* but soon took up position for his right-winger to take the corner kick. He pointed to his forwards and half backs who had moved up to their appropriate positions in readiness for the kick. Then he winked to his winger to lift the ball right up into the air over the goalmouth. The referee blew his whistle. The winger obliged Mr Agomuo with a perfectly placed high kick. It was all his now. He did not need to jump to head the ball goal wards. It hit a startled defender and bounced back into play. The usual scramble started again, with kicks, miskicks and stamping around the goal-mouth.

Mr Agomuo sensibly drew back so that he could have elbow-room and be well sighted if the ball came his way. Soon the ball rolled out of the confusion towards him, and he let go another furious kick from close range. This time his luck held out. The ball felled Gregory, who was still running around aimlessly and carried on into the goal.

His boys were *ecstatic*. All of them, including the goalkeeper, crowded round to congratulate him. "Well done, Sir... Thank you, Sir.... You've saved us, Sir.' All his boys, that is, excluding Gregory who was still flat on his back; and the truth was that it was Gregory who 'scored' that goal as Mr Agomuo tried to explain to his boys. "The last person who touched the ball before it went into the goal was Gregory," he said.

Then they had to see if Gregory was still alive. Everyone crowded around him. The spectators came down too. The referee could not chase them off. Gregory clutched his abdomen with both hands as two teachers carried him off on an improvised stretcher. The game was held up until the field was cleared of *gesticulating* spectators. It was soon obvious that Gregory could not play again, and a substitute was asked for by Mr Agomuo. Three reserves were standing by for each team as was usual in friendly matches. In fact it was a surprise that casualties had not begun coming off until so late in the game.

Gregory's replacement turned out to be Frederick, the 'old man' of Standard Two, who was hard of hearing. He could hear the bang of the football all right, and was quite a useful player. He ran onto the field, vest and *all*, with much exaggerated limbering up all the way. He took the inside left position, and the Second XI forward line stood back for the First XI to kick off after that goal. The Second XI, heartened by their first goal and strengthened by a player clearly less tired than the rest, quickly regained control of the game and mounted a raid on the opposing goal.

Frederick was the spearhead of the attack, and Mr Agomuo, at last seeing someone who seemed likely to break through, fed him with good passes. Soon Frederick was within striking distance of the goal, having dribbled round the flagging defenders and exchanged a couple of short passes with his center forward. Then he was brought down in one of the more characteristic do-or-die tackles in the penalty area. Again the crowd yelled it's unanimous decision: "Penalty! Penalty-y-y!" The referee had already blown for it, and the linesman's flag had also signalled. Mr Obiako ran in from near the touch-line to give an additional warning tug at the ear of the culprit. Since Gregory had been felled by that mighty kick, the referee had been keeping a respectable distance from Mr Agomuo's firing line; hence he had to run in from near the touch-line to supervise the penalty. He walked his measured twelve steps from the goal-line and marked the spot with his heel. Then he withdrew to the side to watch the kick being taken.

As expected by his team and feared by his opponents, Mr Agomuo took the ball and placed it on the penalty 'spot' in readiness to take the kick himself. Thereupon the First XI players protested against his taking the kick, and their goal-keeper calmly walked away from between the posts. The goalkeeper did not want to be murdered from *point blank range* by Mr Agomuo, and his team supported him. Mr Agomuo's boys argued that he must take the kick. The dispute warmed up with such gesticulation and possibly worse to follow. This was the real thing at last football! Real football was a fight, not a friendship.

But Mr Agomuo gave a big laugh and sportingly offered not to take the kick. He told his boys that nothing was at stake, and the game was only being played to entertain the Headmaster. The referee thanked him, as there would have been no justification in forbidding him to take the kick, as he was a member of the team. The First XI goalkeeper returned to his post. Mr Agomuo instructed his center forward on how to take the kick. The crowd watched with bated breath as the center forward walked back almost to the center circle to begin his run up for the kick. The referee blew. The goal-keeper crouched. The center forward ran full speed, and then, Wham! The ball soared high over the crossbar to the anguished: "O-o-o-oh!" from his team-mates and from the crowd. Mr Agomuo's boys resumed the *agitation* that the kick should be re-taken by him. He silenced them. The First XI players were jubilant. The referee indicated a goal kick, and the game was continued.

Five minutes to go, the First XI still 2-1 up, Christian and his mates carried the battle up again. They tried a mid-field thrust, keeping the ball on the ground, but found Mr Agomuo impossible to pass. They tried their flanking *manoeuvre* again and promptly earned a corner on the left. This was taken quickly and Mr Agomuo headed the ball out for another corner on the same side. By this time the entire First XI, apart from the goalkeeper, was massed on the second XI half of the field. Frederick, the late substitute, was the only Second XI player taking part in the wall formation in front of their goal. He was limping slightly from that tackle and lurked about the center circle in line with the First XI left back who had not come as far forward as the other defenders.

As the second corner was taken, it was Mr Agomuo again who intervened, clouting the ball skywards to the mid-field. Frederick and the full back ran together to head it, missed, and the ball landed between them and the goal-keeper who had come far out from his goal. Frederick recovered first, trapped the ball at the second bounce, tapped it past the outstretched hands of the goalkeeper, side-stepped him and ran towards the ball and the empty goal. Everybody went after Frederick the goal-keeper, the full back and the remainder of both teams scattering from the throng near the opposite goal. The crowd roared their encouragement. Mr Agomuo held his breath, praying that Frederick should not, like himself or his entire forward, shoot too hard to control the ball.

Frederick needed no praying for. He kept calm and straight, and as the *stampede* and noise behind built up to its peak, he ran the ball coolly into the goal for the equalizer. Then, with very little emotion, he picked it up, tucked it under his arm, rounded the right upright post, and ran back towards the center spot. He did not get there on foot, being swept off his feet and chaired by his exultant comrades to the center. Some cries of: "Off side" from the First XI was ignored by the refcree. The din took time to die down.

Two minutes to go, and everyone knew the orthodox tactics for this stage of the game to keep the ball with the spectators *if* possible. It was no time to risk raids or dribbling in mid-field. No one would risk losing by attempting to win now. So as soon as Christian kicked off again, completely bemused by the rough luck that had whittled away his glorious first-half

two-goal lead, someone in the Second XI
kicked the ball high over the touch-line into the
crowd. Following the throw in, the ball was
again kicked out of touch. And so it went on,
the game petering out tamely to a dull and
uneventful end -a sad *finale* to a game, which
had been marked earlier by *pluck* and intuition,
if not by polish and imagination.

14

'Wrestling Jacob'

The end of term examinations started on the following Monday. The examination week had always been a *nightmare* to most pupils. It made them more sober than all the caning in the world. The teachers on the other hand got a tremendous kick out of making the examinations seem more *harrowing* than a torture chamber. This week was no different. On Monday, school attendance was one hundred per cent. Few people dared to come late. Even Ishmael was on time.

The Headmaster *hobbled* with the aid of a stick, the only genuine casualty from that football match played in his honour. Mr Mozie,

the Headmaster-*designate,* took the Assembly
in his less demonstrative but still effective way.
He took them swiftly through the drill, and
within minutes everyone was in the Assembly
Hall ready for morning prayers and the
announcements. The only announcement of
note was the grim reminder that the
examinations were being crammed into three
days instead of the usual one-week. This, it was
explained, was in order to leave two days free
for final rehearsals and other arrangements for
the concert due to be held on Friday night.

On that Monday morning Friday night
sounded an *eternity* away. But the worst was
soon over. Wednesday afternoon came, and the
school buzzed back to life games, pranks,
disputes over accounts of the football match,
fights over other trifles, plans for the coming
holidays and for Easter. The holiday mood had
already set in by Thursday morning. Rehearsals

followed the morning Assembly and prayers. Improvised costumes for the plays were gathered or made secretly in every case to prevent rival groups from knowing what each group was preparing.

Miss Chima had been trying to gather large pieces of white wrapping paper through her children in the Infant classes, following Mr Obiako's instruction that she would help the children with their two plays. What an *assortment* of material they brought-brown tobacco wrappers, crumpled posters, sticky soap wrappers, cardboard, cigarette foil! She *discarded* most of what they brought and went herself to the shops to ask for decent wrapping paper. The Manager of W.A.T.C. obliged Miss Chima with rolls and rolls of crisp white wrapping-paper. She got more than she needed, and felt sorry that she had put her children to so much trouble before thinking of going to the shops herself.

She and her children *monopolized* the Church hall, which was their classroom. There, they cut up the paper into appropriate patterns for their main play, and threaded pieces of string through holes *snipped* with scissors.

Other groups prepared and rehearsed in the other classrooms or outside in the playground or in the handwork shed. In and around the classrooms noise and activity reigned, but in their houses the teachers had the peace they wanted to mark the examination papers.

Mr Mozie had taken a personal interest in the concert to ensure that it would be a great success. He arranged that the monitors should submit their plays to a panel of teachers, headed by Mr Ibe and including Mr Okehi and Miss Chima. The panel met the monitors on

Thursday afternoon and drew up the programme for the concert, bearing in mind the length and likely appeal of each play. After Mr Mozie examined and approved the programme, Miss Chima was asked to write out a number of copies.

Friday morning was taken up with preparing the stage and arranging the chairs for the teachers and the invited guests, and the benches for the pupils and the remaining visitors. The Headmaster announced that the afternoon was to be free so that everyone would have enough time to prepare for the concert. Roll-call would be at seven. The concert would begin at half past seven.

The curtain-raiser was a popular *ballad*: 'A friend Better than a Brother' sung as a *duet* by two Standard Four boys. Soon their voices were drowned when practically the whole audience joined in unasked. At the end they bowed, got a good round of applause, and skipped off the stage while the boys working the curtains *pulled like mad* to run their curtains along the rusty overhead wires. One boy ran through first and then dashed across in front of the stage to help his companion pull his unruly half across. This drew much greater applause than the ballad singing.

While one of the curtain boys dashed off to *report to* the stage-manager, Mr Ibe, about the curtains, the audience held a lively discussion on the situation.

"Curtains are always very troublesome," someone remarked.

"I know, they're really terrible. Trust them to *let people down* when a concert *is* being staged for the great H.M.," another agreed heartily.

"Never mind, they'll be all right. All they need is a little more oil so as to run like that!" a knowledgeable third person comforted, snapping his fingers to show how the curtains would run after oiling.

"The teachers should have oiled them beforehand to stop them misbehaving and spoiling the show," the first speaker came in again.

"How do you know they didn't?" the third speaker asked.

And so it went on. The curtains might easily have been *animate* objects the way motives and reactions were happily attributed to them by members of the audience. When the curtains parted again, the stage was in darkness. The very bright pressure lamp from the Headmaster's house, which had stood on a high stand in one corner, had been removed. The three other kerosene lanterns, which had also helped to *illuminate* the stage, were gone.

A little boy stood there alone in the darkness. A spotlight played on his face. He wore what was obviously a priest's collar on his tunic and held a big book in his hand. He bowed stiffly from the waist and received a subdued applause, the audience still feeling uncertain about this *eerie* scene. This young actor rose from his bow, his face and hands showing one more in the spotlight. Then he announced in a piping voice without looking into the open book in his hand: "Our lesson is taken from the book of Genesis, Chapter 32 verses 1 to 32." He made another courteous bow, and disappeared into the darkness of the stage. The spotlight did not follow him. It moved back a short distance on the stage and was joined by a second spotlight from the opposite side of the stage. Together both spotlights picked up a man *swathed* in rich oriental robes, sleeping under a tree, with a piece of rock for his pillow. His long matchet lay beside his pillow.

Out of the darkness of the stage, a voice rang out loud and clear, "And Jacob went on his way, and the angels of God met him."

'And Jacob went on his way and the angels of God met him.

205

Then there was silence. The spotlights still played on the sleeping man. The audience sat *entranced*. There was not a whisper to be heard. The deathly silence was broken by the snoring of the sleeping man. Then slowly, ever so slowly, the spotlights moved and picked up one angel after another as they passed by the sleeping man and up a ladder which led through the fanlights into 'heaven' (the vestry). Each angel was decked in white clothes, a white skull cap or scarf, and white paper wings which crackled softly with each movement. There seemed to be scores of these angels. The spotlights picked up each one of them, but did not play on any for a moment longer than necessary to watch them disappear into 'heaven'.

The hold when this drama had on the audience was reflected in their utter silence.

Only an occasional stifled cough or a controlled sneeze showed that the audience was still there.

The last and most beautiful of the angels came into view and stood looking at the sleeping man. The spotlights swept forwards and backwards between the face of the angel and the face of the sleeping man. The sleeping man stirred. Then he woke up, stood up, and began wrestling with the angel. Out of the darkness again came the loud clear voice: "And Jacob wrestled with an angel until the (breaking of the day."

The wrestling went on, and on, and on. Neither the angel nor the man said a word. The angel's wings crackled with the *exertion*. A sigh here, a deep moan there, were all that could be heard from the audience.

After a long time, the darkness of the stage
was pierced gently by rays of light from one
side of the stage.

Then the angel sang:

"Wrestling Jacob, let me go,

Wrestling Jacob, let me go,

Wrestling Jacob, let me go

And, the man answered,

"Till you bless my spirit I'll not let you go,

Till you bless my spirit I'll not let you go,

Till you bless my spirit I'll not let you go;

I will not let you go."

The wrestling ended. The stage was getting
light. From somewhere on that stage but still
not visible to the audience, the angel's clear

voice came in for the last time: "And the angel blessed Jacob, and called him Israel."

The curtains were drawn across. This time they *cooperated*. The audience broke into thunderous applause and began singing Wrestling Jacob' which they knew very well, but had never seen acted.

The voice from the darkness was that of Miss Chima. 'Wrestling Jacob' was her children's play, her own play in fact. She had produced it, rehearsed with them, and made their costumes wings and all. She must have been very pleased with her children for their wonderful performance.

After 'Wrestling Jacob', the rest of the evening was a comparative *flop*. There was a couple of marriage plays with the familiar haggling over the bride prices, the fattening room customs in preparation for the wedding, the wasteful banqueting on the wedding day, and then the sobering *anti-climax* of the down-to-earth realities of marriage, including mother-in-law problems and other headaches.

There was also a court scene depicting the British District Officer-*cum*-Magistrate presiding, the Police Sergeant and the court interpreter *playing havoc with* both sides in the dispute. It was all *drab*, unexciting stuff, embodying slight modifications of commonplace themes.

The only other play which excited the audience in general and the pupils in particular was one entitled: 'Grammar School Grammar'. It was acted out two Standard Five boys. One was dressed humbly in the school uniform white tunic and brown khaki shorts with his hair close cropped and parted on the left. The other was haughtily attired, the collar of his white shirt turned up, the sleeves buttoned down at the wrists and his hands thrust deep into the pockets of his baggy white trousers. An assortment of fountain pens and pencils peeped from his shirt pocket and his hair was combed high and parted in the middle. The learned Grammar School boy who turned out to be Gregory, the Second XI footballer, was teaching the 'Primary School boy' how the simple quotations they learnt in Primary School sounded in Grammar School *parlance*. The *dialogue* went something like this:

"How would you say... This is the house that Jack built?"!

"Oh that's easy... This is the domiciliary edifice erected by Jack."

There was applause from the audience.

"What of.... Too much of anything is bad?"
"Well,... Superabundance of any performance is detrimental to the performer."

More applause.

"And ... A nod is as good as a wink to a blind horse?"

"Now, let's think ... A slight inclination of the cranium (you follow) is as adequate as a spasmodic movement of one ocular organ (are you with me?) towards an equine quadruped devoid of its visionary capacity (Okay?)."

The boy nodded. The audience broke into an uproar. Pupils clapped and stamped, and shrieked and shouted. This was the sort of thing they enjoyed. There were shouts of: "More! More!! from the audience. After the noise *subsided,* Gregory and his friend resumed their dialogue until their stock of sayings was exhausted, each exchange being greeted with an applause which varied with the length of the words used.

At the end they bowed, the curtains closed and parted again as if for a curtain-call, but there had not been one. Gregory stood there alone. His friend had disappeared. He bowed again, then asked: "Can I tell you a simple story?"

From the audience a voice called out: "Tell us about that football match." This brought a prolonged roar from the audience.

"Oh no, not that one. I'll tell you one more amusing than that:

"Once upon a time in a school not far from here, an unmarried teacher employed a houseboy who could neither read nor write. On the following market day, the teacher, whom we shall call Mr X, drew up a list of articles of food he wanted from the market and handed it to his new house-boy whom we shall call Y. Before he handed it over, however, he read out the

213

contents to Y, hoping he would remember them. The list read:

Yams	6d,	Gari 3d,	
Meat	6d,	Fish 3d,	
Oil	1d,	Salt 1/2d	

and so on until he got to a Total: 1s 9d. He told Y that if he had any difficulty with any item, he must show the list to any educated person around and ask him to read it for him. Finally, he handed two shillings to the boy, emphasizing that he expected a change of three pence, and sent Y on his way."

Up to this point, no one had seen the joke in such a commonplace story. Gregory paused for breath while the audience showed their restlessness, and then he resumed: Y was soon on his way to join the other house-boys from the school compound on their way to the market. Only one thing worried the happy new boy and that was that his master had not helped him further by arranging the items strictly in descending order of costliness. He was determined to seek help as soon as he got to the market and then buy the articles in that order.

At lunch time Y was not back. Most of the other houseboys had returned. New boys were always so *daft,* that was understandable. Mr X had lunch with his next door neighbour and friend who had helped to find him the boy. His friend assured him that his new boy would be all right as time went on; boys from their part of the country being noted for their *humility* and industry. But his friend's houseboy shook Mr X by telling him that he and some other boys had seen Y heading for the shops soon after they arrived in the market. Shops, Mr X pondered: 'What could the fool have been going to the shops for when all the articles on the list could be bought from the market more cheaply?'

Night came, and Y was still nowhere to be seen. Mr X was now genuinely worried, not for Y's safety, but for his money shillings! For dinner he had to *scrounge* again from his friend who was himself beginning to doubt the wisdom of his assurances about *Y's* reliability. Had that fool *embezzled* his friend's money? That would be awful! If the boy did not turn up that night, he would send for his father the following day. He would not let the boy get away with it.

Another house-boy, who returned from the market as it was closing in the evening, reported seeing Y going in the direction of the main town, still hugging an empty basket.

At eight o'clock Mr X and his friend were relaxing in easy chairs in his friend's backyard, trying to recover from their heavy dinner.

Ther suddenly, through the inter-communicating door between the two teachers' houses, the disheveled figure of Y *skulked* in. He looked *a picture of misery*, and was in fact wee-ing. He clutched a piece of paper in one hand, and something else in the other, his shopping basket, still empty.

Mr X sprang to his feet and bawled at Y: 'Goodness gracious, boy, what have you been doing?

'Sir, I couldn't find it anywhere.' He moaned.

Couldn't find what?' Mr X bawled more loudly. Then, stepping forward, he forced the boy's hand open and took the precious two shillings which were still intact. Feeling relieved now, he resumed his seat before calling: Now, come nearer, you fool, and tell us what you have been up to.'

'Sir, today I found out how big this town is. First I went to the W.A. T. C. and they said they didn't have it. Then I went to the N.M.V, and they too didn't have it. At Miller Brothers, they said it was out of stock, and in some of the smaller shops, they said they had never heard of it, and ....'

Heard of what, you blockhead?' Mr X yelled.

By this time the whole school compound had gathered. The teacher drew up chairs and sat with Mr X and his friend while their respective house-boys sneaked in and hid with others in the darkness of the kitchen or behind the doors. Everyone had heard a bit about Y's wanderings.

The poor boy resumed his story:

'When I returned to the market, I went through the big stalls clothes, hardware, cooking utensils and *crockery*, but none of them had it. Late in the afternoon, I was about to give it up and buy the other things when someone suggested some rich merchant in town was bound to have it. I decided to make a last attempt and then to return to the market in time to buy the rest of the things. But I lost my way and by the time I got to the man's house it was nearly seven o'clock. He was truly rich. He sold clothe, gun powder, plates, tobacco, stockfish....'

Mr X interrupted again to comment to his friend: "Honestly, this new *find* of yours must be mad. What is this *twaddle* all about?"

Sir," the boy broke in, "he said he had run out of it, but would order it from Port Harcourt if you wanted him to, that is if you ask him yourself.'

'Asked him for what, boy for what?'

'For this one,' Y said, opening up the paper and pointing. Mr X's friend out of curiosity lifted the lamp to see what the fool was pointing at.

"TOTAL!' He called out at the top of his voice.

"TOTAL! That's what the buffoon has been going round the shops and market all day trying to buy". He *reeled* with laughter, to the accompaniment of everyone around, teachers and houseboys alike.'

By this time, Gregory's long-suffering audience at last had something to laugh about, and they went wild.

At the end of the concert, Mr Offor took the platform. He thanked Mr Mozie, the Headmaster-designate, all the other teachers and the pupils for a wonderful evening. He then announced before taking prayers, as if to emphasize that he was still at the helm, that on Saturday morning all classes were to assemble, clear up the mess of the concert, prepare the hall for Sunday service, and put their classrooms and surroundings in order. He threatened that any class, which failed to put its classroom in order, would not be given their examination results, and that any pupil who was absent would get such a hiding that would be unable to sit down throughout the four week's holidays. They knew that he meant every word he said.

15

Holiday is Coming

The last week of term came. Mr Offor was putting the finishing touch to his handing over notes. He wrote these notes more for record purposes. He was friendly with his *successor*, Mr Mozie, the wide *disparity* in their ages notwithstanding, and *had taken time* over the past few weeks to *acquaint* Mr Mozie with the processes of administering the school, the problems facing the school, and the prospects for the future. He gave him the history of the school from its earliest days and various hints on the tactics of handling various people; the townspeople, fellow teachers, problem pupils, the big *burly* Supervisor of Schools, Mr Dewar.

His handing over was altogether friendly, *with a touch of* fatherliness.

For the pupils, end-of-term *sloth* had set in. Few came to school with their school bags. On the other hand, slates were not so readily abandoned because for those who still used them they came in handy for self-defence, as even the holiday mood had not abolished fighting. Most pupils came for the games and pranks and jokes, and the fear of punishment also kept attendance from slumping. Furthermore, three events during the last week promised some excitement or two events certainly. The third event, the examination results, was awaited with mixed feelings. The two other events were the women's folk dance in honour of Mr and Mrs Offor on Wednesday afternoon and the Headmaster's actual send-off on Friday morning.

It was during the folk-dance that Stanislaus turned up again like a bad penny. The dance was being held in the school square. Mr Mozie was helping with the *organization* of the various groups of dancers. There were three age groups adolescent girls *bedecked* with short silk skirts, silk headgear jingling beads; young married women less gaudily *attired* in ankle-length wrappers, loose blouses and silk head ties; and then older "women with much less interest in bright colors but nevertheless loaded with expensive beads round their necks and ivory bangles and more beads round their wrists. Each group had some advantage over the others.

Adolescent girls bedecked with short silk skirts, silk headgears and jingling beads.

The adolescents had youth, young married women beauty and serenity, and the older women wealth. How these factors matched with the art of dancing was yet to be seen. The adolescent girls had just finished one of their dances and been applauded off the square. Mr Mozie was instructing the attendants on how and when to lead in the next group, when Stanislaus *eased his up* and asked in his smoothly courteous language: "Could I have a word with you, Sir, if you please."

"What is it?" Mr Mozie asked.

"Well there is a rumour in town that the people will petition against your appointment as H.M. Have you heard it?" Stanislaus asked, scarcely raising his voice above a whisper.

"I won't discuss the matter with you, thank you." Mr Mozie told him calmly, and went on to see about the dancing.

Stanislaus *was* at a loss. All he wanted was a 'yes' or 'no' answer, to see if Mr Mozie knew anything about his plans. No wonder people complained that this man was unapproachable.

The dancing went on *without a hitch.* Mrs Offor earned the loudest applause by stepping out, without rehearsal, to dance first with the young married women and later with the rich older women. The girls clamoured for her to dance with them too, and as she walked out to oblige them, they garlanded her with all their beads and spread their silk head-bands for her on the dancing arena. The dancing was altogether a joyous occasion.

At a meeting later that day, where Stanislaus was *to* read to the Committee men his draft of what he called an *addendum* to the original petition, he still *held the men. under his spell* in spite of his personal uneasiness about Mr Mozie. He read:

'In view of the most recent developments, culminating in the *foisting* on the school and Church and people of Amanzu, without their consultation or consent, a young Headmaster with neither matrimonial achievement nor apparently matrimonial intentions; a young man alleged to be obsessed with books Cane and with reading; alleged to suffer from *temerity* of and aversion to corporal punishment for the correct education of the pupils; alleged to be softly disposed to the said pupils and alleged to be disdainful Bon of and incompatible with the people of Amanzu, we, the chosen and honourable representatives of the people, do hereby register our deep and lasting apprehension over this appointment, this being a prelude to a petition which will be penned when, as we anticipate, not with malice, but with intuition, the said appointment turns out to be the *unmitigated* catastrophe we believe it to be."

He expanded this scheme in similarly ver*bose* paragraphs, and followed it with the long list of the Committee men and their signatures or marks. They accepted his draft without much criticism. They did not see anything wrong or *two-faced* in adding this warning, which they were confused into believing was not a petition as such, while at the same time arranging the grand send-off, which Mr Offor was already having. In fact they almost looked at the 'testimonial' as the final item on the send-off programme. It was to be sent to the Reverend William Jones during the following week. The Committee had already made good their promises about the various presents. The women's dance had come off magnificently. The arrangements for the hiring of the lorry on Friday had been made. There has not been one hitch in any of their plans. They had cause to be satisfied.

Friday morning came, and with it the final acts of the term's drama. Every pupil attended school, but not even the keenest monitors thought of coming along with anything apart from the clothes they stood in. Goodwill was the mood of the day. Monitors and other pupils were friends again. The school compound rang with the whistling and humming of the song, which was the pupils' 'Victory march':

Holiday is coming,

No more morning bells,

No more teachers' calls.

Scholars goodbye,

Teachers keep

While I go to spend

My Jolly holidays.'

The Assembly, taken by Mr Mozie, was peaceful. The prayers were brief. The only announcements were that after roll call and the examination results in the various classes, the desks were to be stacked up in the classrooms, the benches were to be brought to the Assembly Hall for Sunday services during the holidays, and then everyone must reassemble in the hall for the bed no Headmaster's speech.

No class had dared to disobey the Head master's orders about work on Saturday following the concert, so no results were withheld. Nevertheless, results were as disastrous as ever, especially in the lower classes. The names of successful pupils were called, and all who did not hear their names knew they had failed. One *consolation* was that there was little time to brood over the results. No reports were issued to take back to parents.

Mr Offor's speech had one theme as usual. After tracing the history of the school from its foundation, he proceeded *to catalogue* all the ways in which the pupils had been a failure. In general they were lazy, untidy, given to lying and truancy. Inside the classrooms, they disobeyed and harassed their teachers and made teaching difficult. They evaded homework and *shirked* schoolwork. Many preferred fishing, trapping and hunting to schooling. Their parents found them as difficult as the teachers, and bad reports from their parents were frequent. They compared unfavourably with pupils from other schools in many spheres of activity. They lost most of their inter-school football matches, came off badly in the Empire Day Athletic competitions, and the school choir had never won the annual District singing contest. Their results in Government Standard Six (First School Leaving Certificate) examinations were *poor*. As for passing entrance examinations to secondary schools, that only happened once *in a blue moon*. They even found passing the entrance examination into the Lower Elementary Teacher Training College difficult. All they seemed keen to do was to become policemen, court clerks and court interpreters because those were the easiest ways of making money quickly.

He and his teachers, he declared, had laboured in vain, working their hearts out to improve the school. As he was now leaving the school, all he could do was to continue to pray that the Almighty in His infinite mercy would hear his cries and mend the pupils' ways.

Far from wanting to hurt his pupils' feelings, the Headmaster made these scathing remarks only *to spur* them on to work harder. To show them the spirit in which he spoke, he made his usual quotation: "The son whom his father loveth, he chideth ...' He was only chiding them, not condemning them.

Then continuing, he said: "I have one final announcement to make.' As he saw so many pupils looking ill at ease, he hastened to add:

"It's nothing terrible. I merely wish to inform you that the lorry, which was hired by the kind people of Amanzu to take me and my family to my new station, is now here. It is at this moment being loaded by the driver and his assistant. These kind people have given us more presents than even the lorry can carry easily. The lorry crew is packing the loads as economically as only they know how. There may be a little room left by the tailboard when they have finished. Some of you might still feel disposed to see us off part of the way, either by jumping on to the tailboard or following on foot. The gesture will be appreciated. You know how readily these lorries break down even when travelling light. This lorry will certainly need some pushing uphill, so I don't want the lazy ones among you. We shall set off at noon."

After that he called the school-parting hymn: 'God be with you till we meet again' and the pupils gave a full-throated and joyous rendering of it.

That was it. The term ended on that prayerful note. But the tune whistled or hummed by those not staying on to join the Headmaster's dust-run was the Victory *march*: 'Holiday is coming'.

The story of: **The Village School** is continued in *Anezi* Okoro's **The Village Headmaster**.